P. C. Doherty was born in Middlesbrough and educated at Woodcote Hall. He studied History at Liverpool and Oxford Universities and obtained a doctorate at Oxford for his thesis on Edward II and Queen Isabella. He is now the Headmaster of a school in North-East London.

His hobbies include films, cycling and Chinese cookery and he lives with his American wife and family near Epping Forest, along with a horse, cat and other sundry animals.

Acclaim for the Hugh Corbett medieval mysteries:

'Wholly excellent, this is one of those books you hate to put down' *Prima*

'I really like these medieval whodunnits' *Bookseller*

'A powerful compound of history and intrigue' *Redbridge Guardian*

'Medieval London comes vividly to life . . . Doherty's depictions of medieval characters and manners of thought, from the highest to the lowest, ringing true' *Publishers Weekly*

'A romping good read' *Time Out*

'Historically informative, excellently plotted and, as ever, superbly entertaining' *CADS*

Satan in St Mary's

P. C. Doherty

HEADLINE

First published in 1986
by Robert Hale Limited

First published in paperback in 1990
by HEADLINE BOOK PUBLISHING

10 9 8 7

ISBN 0 7472 3492 2

Printed and bound in Great Britain by
Mackays of Chatham PLC, Chatham, Kent

HEADLINE BOOK PUBLISHING
A division of Hodder Headline PLC
338 Euston Road
London NW1 3BH

INTRODUCTION

A savage, cold wind had sprung up just after dark. It stirred and rippled the black water of the Thames, hit the moored ships and sent them moving and straining at their ropes. The decaying corpses of three river pirates twisted and twirled in the wind to the creak of the scaffold overhead. Ghostly dancers grimly turning to macabre music. The wind pierced the alleys and rutted tracks of the city, freezing the mud and ordure, driving deeper into the darkness those human predators of the shadows who might still be hunting for any unfortunate abroad on such a dark and miserable night.

The church of St. Mary Le Bow stood alone and desolate, its carved brick and woodwork open to the wind. The cemetery which surrounded it whispered and murmured with sound as leaves and branches were scornfully cast around by the wind as it bent and shook the flimsy wooden crosses of the dead. Inside the church, it was cold and dark, the wind slammed close a loose shutter and then continued to play its distant eerie music in the cracks and crevices of the crumbling masonry. The place was deserted and quiet except for the scurrying patter of the occasional rat and the slow dripping of rain water through a tear in the roof as it trickled down the mildewed wall forming a green dank puddle at its base. In the sanctuary, before the high altar, a man sat bolt upright in the Blessed Chair. His soft, plump hands clutched the carved wood as if he was reassuring himself that as long as he sat in that chair then he had found sanctuary and was protected by all the power, temporal and spiritual, of the Church. Yet he was afraid, his large protuberant eyes stared into the darkness, searching for Them, wondering if They would come. He had sinned grievously in being one of Them, he had sinned grievously in killing one of Them and They would not forget that. Nor would God. The man's fingers felt the carved letters which ran along the arms of the chair – '*Hic est terribilis locus*' – this is a terrible place, the House of God where Angels walked and worshipped before the White Body of Christ. Yet here too, he had sinned, most horribly, committed an abominable act in the hope it would ease his terror and despair. He thought of the knife which had brought him here, it had slipped so easily into the soft throat of the man. Like something from a dream, he remembered it going in soft and smooth like a spoon into cream. He had not meant to do it, yet it was done, and now he was a murderer, a fugitive from the King's Justice and from something much more terrifying. He jumped as a bird or bat was driven by the wind into one of the long shuttered windows above him. He stared up deep into the dark alcove and then, hearing a faint sound from the far end of the church, he turned his head back slowly, feeling the hair on the nape of his neck rise in horror at what it might be. They had come, standing with a torch spluttering above them. They seemed to have emerged, hooded and cloaked from the darkness. They stood, a group of black evil crows in the pool of light thrown by their torches and then began to move soundlessly towards him. The man moaned in terror and sank deeper into the chair oblivious to the hot wetness between his fat thighs. His hands gripped the wood, his head fast against the back of the chair as his eyes darted to and fro. There must be, surely, he thought, some way of escape from the hell advancing towards him. He wanted to run but he could not move, perhaps the wine! If only his legs and arms were not so heavy, he could escape the terrors now approaching him.

One

Edward, King of England and Duke of Aquitaine, sat in the small sparse chamber of his palace at Westminster. Few people knew he was in the capital for he had only returned at the urgent insistence of his Chancellor, Robert Burnell, Bishop of Bath and Wells. Exhausted after his journey, Edward crouched over a small, fiery red brazier, his cloak wrapped about him, trying to ignore the cold wind which battered insistently on the wooden shutters. Edward eventually rose and crossed the room to ensure they were closed fast; it was dark outside, the city and river concealed by thick mists, only the moaning of the wind and the howling of some street dog cut through the eerie silence. The King shivered and jumped as a rat rustled the herb-strewn rushes. A room with too many dark corners, the King thought, hidden from the torches flickering in their sconces on the wall. "Shadows everywhere," Edward muttered to himself and returned to crouch over the brazier and examine the shadowy ghosts who haunted his own soul. First, there was his father, Henry, pleasure-loving, aesthetic, eager to please, only concerned about his own comforts and those of his favourites: soft-skinned, soft-spoken, Henry's only interest had been the building of his precious abbey here at Westminster.

There were other more threatening figures: the de

Montforts; flaxen-haired Simon and his arrogant, aggressive boys, with their smiling faces and treacherous hearts. Once Simon had been a close friend, Edward had even joined him against his own father, the King, in order to build a better Community of the Realm, but those dreams turned into nightmares. Henry was a poor king but de Montfort and the other barons were tyrants seeking their own good. Simon had been the worst, linked to Satanic covens, with their filthy, secret rites which his damnable family had picked up in the soft, luxurious provinces of southern France. Even dead, Edward morosely thought, de Montfort's hand stretched from the grave across the years to haunt him. Indeed, the King often wondered if de Montfort was really dead or still alive, leading his secret covens, organizing the assassinations which pursued Edward like some savage, well-trained hunting dogs. Edward looked down at the white furrowed scar on his right hand. "De Montfort must be dead!," he whispered to the brazier, "Killed at Evesham years ago." The King stared into the blazing coals, the red flames reminding him of that fiery, murderous day among the green meadows and apple-strewn fields of Evesham some twenty years before. He and his troops had advanced against Simon with banners snapping and flapping in the breeze. The summer day had quickly died as a thunderstorm suddenly swept the skies, the crashing thunder and flashes of lightning drowning the pounding hooves of his mailed cavalry as they charged the small, trapped rebel army. Edward still remembered, from all the battles he had ever fought in, the moment of impact at Evesham as he crashed through Simon's troops, drenching his sword in rebel blood. At the end Simon had stood alone, fully clothed in mail armour, he bestrode the corpses of his fallen bodyguard, taunting the royal troops to close with him. Edward had sat and watched the rebel leader being overborne. At that precise moment the storm had suddenly ended and the rays of a thin sun caught the blood seeping through the gaps of Simon's armour, making it sparkle like cascading rubies. They hacked Simon's body to bits. Edward shuddered, slightly fearful at what he had ordered in the heat of battle, for he had instructed his men to feed the battered remains of Simon's corpse to a pack of starving wolfhounds. "Yes," Edward muttered. "Simon must be dead."

The King stared round the deserted chamber. If Simon was dead, he thought despairingly, then his followers were certainly not, organizing covens, plotting to kill him by poison, dagger, sword, mace or arrow through assassins by day or night, at home or abroad. Abroad! Edward gazed into the darkness. He remembered Acre in Palestine where, some eight years after his victory at Evesham, he and his queen, Eleanor, were on crusade trying to impose unity amongst the petty principalities of Outremer. He had thought that at least there he would be safe but the assassins struck. A Christian hermit asked for an audience and Edward had nodded his agreement, his mind on other matters. The man, grovelling and verminous like many of his kind, entered and stood in the shadows of the tent. Edward recalled seeing him take something from his sleeve and only reacted when the sharp stiletto knife came streaking for his heart. Edward had sidestepped, crying out, "Treason!", his guards burst in and cut the man down but the dagger and its poison were lodged in his arm. If it had not been for Eleanor the poison would have raced for his heart but she had immediately cut the wound and sucked out the poison herself.

Edward rose and poured a cup of wine. Eleanor! He should be with her now, enjoying her silken, warm brown body, not sitting in this deserted chamber brooding over the past. He sipped the wine. If only the past would die, leave him alone. He had so much to do but de Montfort and his secret societies persistently hounded him. "Go back to your grave, Simon!," he whispered fiercely but the only answer was the darkness and the insistent whine of the wind. Edward rose and peered through the shutters. Beneath the swirling river mist, his capital lay quiet, though Edward knew different. Simon's followers, the covens with their constant plots and secret plans were gathering there scheming murder, treason and rebellion. Rats scampering about in their holes and runnels of the city Edward thought and, whatever they were plotting, was coming to a head like a boil full with yellow pus. His spies had told him this. Everything pointed to an un-avoidable crisis. They had already begun to act; the suicide in St. Mary Le Bow was, the King reasoned, somehow linked to these rebels, and it was time that Burnell, his wily old Chancellor, flushed these traitors out into the light of day and destroyed them.

There was a knock at the door, it opened and the man Edward had been thinking about waddled into the room. Robert Burnell, Bishop of Bath and Wells and Chancellor of England, sketched the briefest of bows to his monarch and heaved himself into the room's one and only chair, dabbing his fat, florid face with the voluminous sleeve of his fur-trimmed gown. "God save your Grace," he almost wheezed, "I cannot understand why you always insist on taking the highest chamber in whatever palace, castle or manor you stay." Edward smiled affectionately. There was little pomp or courtly graces between himself and his Chancellor. They were old friends united against old enemies. He trusted Burnell as he did his own right arm. The Chancellor, despite his fat pompous appearance, had a brilliantly sharp and cunning brain, whether it be drafting a legal document or searching out the King's enemies, both at home and abroad.

"You know, my Lord Burnell," the King jibed, "why I always stay in the highest chamber. It would be a clever assassin who could scale these walls or bypass the guards on the narrow staircases outside. You have heard from your spy?"

Burnell shook his head. "No," he replied slowly. "I don't think I ever will. His body was taken from the Thames this morning. His throat was cut from ear to ear!"

Edward snorted in annoyance. "So, the conspiracies continue!"

"Yes," Burnell replied. "However, we do know that there are covens here in the city plotting treason and rebellion."

"And the incident at the church of Saint Mary Le Bow could be part of it?" the King asked.

"Yes," his Chancellor murmured.

"How was your spy discovered?" enquired Edward.

Burnell shrugged. "It is only supposition on my part," he answered slowly. "But I suspect that there is a spy at the heart of the very chancery!"

"You mean here?" Edward exclaimed. "A royal clerk involved with the followers of de Montfort, plotting treason against his king?"

Burnell nodded. "That is the only way," he replied firmly, "my spy could have been discovered. Somebody, one of a few clerks, passed on confidential information he should not have. It may not be that he is a conspirator but simply did it for greed, for a purse of gold. If he is caught," Burnell concluded bitterly, "then rest assured he will hang just as high as the rest."

"Then what now?" said the King. "What shall we do now?" He walked over to his Chancellor and patted him on the shoulder.

"Earlier," Edward said softly, "I compared these conspirators, these rebels, the scum of this city to rats, I see you, my Lord Bishop, as my rat-catcher. You must run these vermin out into the open."

The Chancellor coughed and cleared his throat. "I have chosen a man," he replied, "another clerk who now serves in the Courts of King's Bench." Burnell stopped speaking and looked fearfully up at the King. "He is, my Lord, probably our last and only hope!"

"Good," the King murmured. "But do not inform him of your suspicions that there could be a spy here in the very Palace of Westminster. After all," he concluded meaningfully, "it could be one of his friends!"

* * *

They always met here, the charnel house of a deserted London church, a rotten mildewed crypt, secretive, closed, hidden from spies and the eyes of the curious. They had intoned their prayer to Lucifer, the Fallen Morning Star, their hands outstretched above a crude stone altar bearing mystical symbols round an inverted cross. Only one torch spluttered and flared against the cold darkness but this revealed nothing of the thirteen hooded figures, the cowls of their cloaks covering their heads, their faces concealed behind crude leather masks. They did not even know each other, only their leader, the Hooded One, silent as ever, was aware of their identities. They were bound by macabre pacts and bloody oaths to destroy the King and create revolt. This was the essence of their being, the link between each of them and they were here to learn how it was to be achieved.

The figure to the right of the Leader's chair began to talk raspingly, his voice muffled by the mask, his words, no more than whispers, echoed round the cold, sinister chamber. "So, it is done," he murmured. "Those who threatened the Grand Design, both the spy and the murderer, are removed, gone to their appointed place."

"No other threat exists?" asked another member of the group.

"Yes and no," the first speaker replied, turning to survey his colleagues one by one. "Our Master," and he turned to bow to the figure in the chair. "Our Master says that the King and his minions have appointed a clerk to investigate the matter. Our spy in the chancery has warned us to be wary of him."

"Why?" one of the group interjected. "What danger does this one man pose?"

The Hooded One held up one hand for silence and beckoned into the shadows. An old woman crinkled and bent with age shuffled forward, looking nervously from side to side as she moved to crouch in the centre of the group. She pushed straggly hair from her skull-like face, plunged her hand into a dirty leather bag she carried with her, and drew out a black, silk-plumed cock, who stirred restlessly in her hand but was unable to protest because of the drugged corn it had been fed. The old woman held the bird up in her hands, bowed first toward the Hooded One and then towards the altar, she mumbled a prayer and bit deeply into the fat plump neck of the cock. Its body jerked furiously and lay limp as the old woman, her mouth smeared with blood, raw flesh and feathers, looked up and stared triumphantly around the group, who had watched the scene so impassively. She sprinkled the blood on the dirty floor, in blasphemous parody of a priest who cleanses his congregation with a rod of hyssop before Mass began. The old hag then knelt and carefully studied the pool of blood which had formed, groaning and muttering to herself. She turned towards the Hooded One. "The man the King has chosen," she croaked, "is indeed dangerous. If he is not stopped, you will not take vengeance on the House of

Plantagenet. The day of deliverance so carefully planned, will never occur. This clerk must be killed!"

The hooded leader listened as if concentrating on something else and bent to whisper to the masked speaker on the right, who turned to address the group. "Let the clerk, whoever he is," he replied, "flounder about. He is just one man. There are many traps. Rest content. He will be stopped." His voice rose arrogantly. "The day of deliverance will come. We will cleanse the country of all kings, bishops, priests and others who lord it over us. Rest content with that!"

The group, sensing that the meeting was over, began to disperse one by one, each bowing to the hooded leader before departing. When they had all left, the speaker turned to the Hooded One and pointed to the old crone who still sat as if in a trance on the beaten dirt floor.

"She waits for her reward," he said. "What shall we give her?"

"She has served her purpose," came the whispered reply. "Cut her throat!"

Two

Hugh Corbett, clerk to the King's Justices in King's Bench, sat huddled in his blankets on the side of his pallet bed. His thin white face under a mass of black wiry hair was strained and pinched with cold. He pulled the blankets around him and then stretched out cold numbed fingers to a small charcoal brazier which was at last beginning to glow, thinning his breath as it hung heavy on the icy air. He was cold and reluctant to wash in the bowl of lukewarm water that a servant had just brought him. He was often teased by his colleagues when they learnt he insisted on washing all his body once a day. He shrugged at the thought, dropped the blankets and, ignoring the cold, began to rub his body with a cloth soaked in the water. A physician, an Arab, who owed a favour, had once informed him that it was a way of limiting infection. He stopped and stared dully at the cloth. Infection! He wondered if anything could have stopped the plague killing his wife and child. A dull ache from long-buried pain sent shivers through his body and he began to dry himself roughly. His wife and child, happy faces, strong healthy bodies, clean-limbed then, in a matter of days, both transformed to stinking, retching shadows as the buboes appeared in pus-filled sores all over their bodies. They were dead almost before he knew it, buried in the quiet churchyard of Alfriston in Sussex.

Ten years, almost ten years, he thought and the pain was still there. He looked down at his body, thin, sinewy and crisscrossed with scars, legacies of his part in King Edward's wars in Wales. He stretched, then turned his arm to look at the long purple scar which ran from shoulder to wrist. He had received it seven, or was it eight, years ago? He had forgotten except that his family were dead and buried long before it happened. He had volunteered to serve in the royal household during the Welsh expedition, hoping perhaps that Death which had missed him when the plague had struck would find him there. He had gone and been in the thick of the fighting as Edward I's armies edged their way up the misty treacherous valleys of South Wales, hunting for Llewellyn's army, frightened of the Welsh who used the misty forlorn marshes and bogs to loose their barbed lethal arrows or spring an ambush. Their wild naked warriors would appear suddenly with their long wicked hunting knives, ready to kill the stragglers or unwary.

One night they had launched a surprise attack on the main English camp looking for the royal pavilion. He had been one of those who had stopped them, fighting desperately outside the very tent of the King, locked in combat with a group of Welsh, whose naked greasy bodies pressed against the line of bodyguards hastily assembled to block their progress. He had stood and scrabbled in the mud, hacking and lashing out, screaming curses until his voice went hoarse. Eventually the Welsh were pushed back and only then had he realized that his left arm was one bloody gash. Of course, the King had been grateful, Edward never forgot a favour or an injury. Hugh's wounds were tended by a royal physician and when he returned to London, he was not too surprised to find he had been given preferment, being appointed a clerk to the Royal Justices in King's Bench. He had been there ever since, drawing up the bills of indenture, filing the conclusions of the court, almost oblivious to the human misery such records contained. Except today. Today would be different and this made him dress hastily while he peered through the cracks in one of the shutters and tried to guess what hour it now was. The bells of a nearby church tolling for Mass had woken him. His appointment was at noon and he believed he still had two hours to make the journey, although the dense fog outside would make the travelling more difficult. He finished dressing, bound a belt with a long leather dagger sheath and small purse around his waist; he drew a thick woollen cloak from the room's one and only chest and left the chamber to make his way down the long winding wooden stairs. He remembered half way down that he had not locked the door and turned to go back but then shrugged. A small garret with a rush strewn floor, simple bed and an almost empty wooden chest would scarcely tempt the most desperate thief. Corbett turned and made his way down into the street.

Outside the morning mist still hung heavy above the noise of the carts. Hugh walked up Thames Street staying in the middle, away from the windows of the overhanging houses from where maids were already dumping the ordure and rubbish of the night so the scavengers or rakers could clear it away. The city fathers had condemned such practices and even appointed surveyors of the streets to fine offenders and kill any animals found rooting in such rubbish. Hugh wrapped his cloak tighter round him and realized such ordinances had been forgotten during the recent revolt. These were dangerous times even during the day, and Hugh's hand beneath his cloak rested on the handle of the long Welsh dagger he kept stuck in his belt. Lawlessness was rife, 'roaring boys', gangs of ruffians roamed the streets and the hue and cry was often raised by horn or voice in a

usually futile attempt to capture some criminal. Certain
areas, like the precincts and graveyard of St. Paul's, were
virtually beyond the law and were now the sanctuary for
every villain, murderer and thief in the capital.

As Hugh moved out of Queenshithe, the city was coming
to life. Eel-sellers, coal-boys, water-sellers and the swarming
perceptive beggars appeared to pursue their flourishing
trade. The wooden fronts of small shops were brought down
and the merchants and tradesmen muffled against the cold
began to tout for business. Corbett ignored them all as he
made his way down to the windswept, bitter cold river and,
at the nearest mooring steps, hired a wherry to take him
through the misty, choppy Thames to Westminster Hall.
The journey was most unpleasant and, by the time he
reached the palace, Corbett almost wished he had walked.
He climbed the steps and crossed a rutted track to the main
causeway which led to the great gabled Palace of
Westminster and the majestic gardens, walls and buildings
of the Abbey. He had been taking the same route for years
but every day, the awesome Abbey Church with its pillars,
arches and towers always caught his breath. A mass of
beautifully carved stone seemingly suspended, fairy-like in
the misty air.

This morning, however, he kept on walking, pushing his
way through the gathering crowds and into the great vaulted
hall of the palace. Here, in various corners and alcoves sat
the different royal courts, each cordoned off, its red-robed
judges, soberly dressed clerks and black-robed lawyers
dispensing judgments and justice. This, as well as the
buildings and rooms around the hall were the King's
government and Corbett's usual place of work but, today, it
was different. He caught the eye of one of the Chancellor's
clerks, showed him the writ and was then led through the
hall and into a small chamber. He immediately dropped to

one knee when he recognized the Chancellor, Robert Burnell, Bishop of Bath and Wells. Small, swathed in red ermine-lined robes, Burnell reminded Hugh of a small cherubim he had seen in a painting in a rich city merchant's house. Yet there was nothing angelic about the large bald head or the hooked nose above thin lips and firm chin, while the narrow, agate-hard eyes were more like those of a hunting dog. These eyes now studied Hugh for a while and then, in a surprisingly soft deep voice, bade him rise and sit on a stool a harassed clerk had brought across before being summarily dismissed from the room.

Once the clerk was gone, closing the door behind him, Burnell rose and sifted through the documents strewn across the table in front of him. Eventually, with a grunt of pleasure, he plucked one from the pile, rolled it up and tossed it over to Hugh. "Read it," he ordered. "Read it now!" Hugh nodded and unrolled the vellum which he immediately recognized as cheap and the scrawled, badly penned writing as something certainly not produced by clerks trained in the royal chancery. It was the report of a coroner's inquest held in Cheapside at the church of St. Mary Le Bow:

"The findings of Roger Padgett, Coroner called to the church of St. Mary Le Bow on the morning of 14th January 1284 to view, in the presence of witnesses called from the ward, the body of Lawrence Duket, goldsmith. It was established that the said Lawrence Duket had killed Ralph Crepyn in Cheapside and fled to the church for sanctuary in the Blessed Chair. It was also established that the said Lawrence Duket out of fear of what he had done, took his own life by hanging himself from a bar near a window in the sanctuary of the said church. The coroner decided that the said Lawrence Duket was a suicide and should be treated as such."

Corbett let the manuscript fall from his fingers on to his lap and stared at the King's Chancellor. "So, a man has committed suicide, my Lord! What is that to me?" The Chancellor grunted and shuffled his huge bulk as if the stuffed cushions he sat on did not protect his soft arse from discomfort.

"Was it suicide?" he asked. "Or was it murder? Duket," he continued, not waiting for an answer, "Duket was a goldsmith and vintner. A man of good family and influential friends. He was also a loyal subject of the King and supported His Highness during the recent troubles." He stopped and looked at Corbett, who knew too well what the "recent troubles" were.

In 1258 almost thirty years ago, civil war had broken out between Simon de Montfort, Earl of Leicester, and Henry III, the present King's father. Indeed, the Lord Edward had first joined the rebels against his father before seeing the wisdom of fighting for a cause which threatened his own future livelihood, namely the crown of England. Edward had rallied behind his father and, after a long bloody civil war, the rebels had been smashed at the Battle of Evesham in August 1265, de Montfort's body being hacked to pieces as if he had been a mad dog.

Edward had then turned his wrath on London which had supported de Montfort, declaring itself a commune, a republic free of the crown. The Radicals, or 'Populares', had taken over the city, flying the black banner of anarchy. They had hunted down and killed those loyal to the crown. Even Queen Eleanor, Edward's mother, was attacked as she tried to leave the city for Windsor. The Populares had ambushed her at London Bridge and pelted her cortège with rocks, sticks and the rotting corpses of dead animals, forcing the Queen to seek sanctuary in St. Paul's Cathedral. Edward never forgave the city for their treatment of his 'blessed' mother and, after his victory at Evesham, returned to the capital to instigate a reign of terror, with all the usual apparatus of spies, torture, prosecutions, quick trials and even more abrupt executions. The city had to forfeit many of its privileges, charters and concessions granted by the Crown during the previous centuries. Edward exacted vengeance and only now, almost twenty years after Evesham, was the King beginning to relax his grip over the city.

The Chancellor had sat and watched Corbett reflect on his words. Burnell was pleased and smiled secretively to himself. He had chosen the right man, a human terrier who would seek the truth, whatever it was and so break the rebellious spirit in the capital. The Chancellor hated untidiness, irregularity and London was all of these. A seething bed of resentment against royal policies and justice where the weeds of rebellion festered and spread. They had to be pulled out by the roots and Corbett would assist in this.

"Well?" Burnell smiled as benevolently as he could, his lips wide displaying a row of rotten blackened stumps.

"Well, Master Corbett, you may ask what this suicide has to do with the troubles faced by His Highness in his governance of this city?" He waited till he caught the deep brooding eyes of the clerk before continuing.

"You know that the King intends to break once and for all the rebellious elements which still fester in the city. The Mayor, Henry Le Waleys, has issued a series of ordinances to bring the city to heel." The Chancellor began to tick off on his fingers the more recent security measures: "Inns and all their inmates are to be registered: all trades and guilds have to register members, anyone over the age of twelve. A new system of watch in every ward of the city: a curfew after dark and confinement in a new prison, the Tun at Cornhill, for those who break it."

The Chancellor stopped and stared at Corbett. The clerk was courteous but those hard, dark eyes showed the

Chancellor that he was not subdued. A moment of doubt made Burnell falter. Was Corbett too hard, too thorough? Corbett, however, had no such doubts about himself. He was waiting for the Chancellor to come to the point and, like any good clerk, knew that when he did, it would need all of his attention. The Chancellor grunted and picked up a cup of mulled wine, drained it and leaned back, more comfortable, as the hot liquid warmed his belly and relaxed his aged body, so tense against the cold. He held the still warm cup between his hands and leaned across the table. "I know you, Master Corbett, with your obedient face and watchful eyes. You may well ask what has this suicide got to do with the King or, indeed, the tangled politics of the city. And," he added, "you are too polite to ask what has it got to do with you, a clerk in the Court of King's Bench?" He put the cup down slowly and continued speaking: "You know that de Montfort, though dead for almost two decades, still has supporters in the city. Well, Ralph Crepyn, the man Duket killed, was one of these. A commoner." The Chancellor stopped and smiled.

"I mean no disrespect to you, Master Corbett, but Crepyn was from the gutter. A sewer rat who used his ability to lend money and arrange shady business dealings to rise to high office in the city. His family were Populares, Radicals, supporters of the dead de Montfort but Crepyn survived the crash and even reached the office of alderman. Here, he ran into opposition from Duket, a goldsmith and also a member of the City Council. Duket resented Crepyn but this turned to hatred when Crepyn lent Duket's sister money at such high interest the silly fool was unable to repay. Crepyn exacted his price. He reduced the loan on one condition, that Duket's sister sleep with him."

Burnell stopped to clear his throat. "Crepyn then proclaimed this to the city and the world, adding spicy details of how Duket's sister had performed in bed. It was this which led to the meeting in Cheapside and Crepyn's death."

The Chancellor shrugged. "We are well rid of Master Crepyn but the King is furious at Duket's death, yet astute enough to use the incident to investigate Crepyn's links with secret rebels as well as the professional thugs of the criminal world."

The Chancellor stopped and passed Corbett a small scroll of vellum tightly bound in the scarlet red ribbon of the royal chancery. "This is your commission, Master Clerk. You are to investigate the circumstances surrounding the death of Duket and report directly to the King through me. You do understand?"

Corbett accepted the scroll and nodded. "Oh," he remarked, "are there records, manuscripts?"

"What do you mean, Corbett?" Burnell asked.

"Well, both men were merchants. Surely they kept horn books, records of their transactions?"

"No," the Chancellor firmly replied. "Duket's records show nothing and Crepyn's disappeared within hours of his death!" He paused. "Anything else?"

Corbett shook his head.

"Good," the Chancellor smilingly concluded. "Then we wish you every success." Burnell would have left it at that but was annoyed at the young clerk's imperviousness. "It is a dangerous task," he added warningly. "These are dark pools you search and the mud and weeds could well drag you down and choke you!"

Three

Corbett spent the greater part of the afternoon taking leave of his colleagues in the court of King's Bench. He knew well that he would not be missed. A stranger, he had many acquaintances but few friends and his temporary referral to a new assignment prompted little or no questioning. It was quite common for clerks to be reassigned to different tasks, a diplomatic mission abroad or, not so popular, an audit of one of the royal manors, or tramping the shires with the King's Justices in Eyre. Corbett removed certain of his belongings from a small leather trunk he kept in one of the record offices and wrapped them in a bundle; a few coins, the ring belonging to his dead wife, a lock of his child's hair, a spoon made out of cow's horn, and certain writing materials.

Burnell had instructed him to begin his assignment immediately and Corbett did not delay. He thought of using his writ to draw monies from the Exchequer but he knew this would be a laborious task. The Exchequer clerks were suspicious of everyone, particularly other clerks. They would make him wait, examine the writ and then sparingly dole out the money. No, he decided, wrapping his cloak round him, he would draw some of his own money from a goldsmith in Cheapside, and then submit his account direct to Burnell. After all, money was no problem to him, he was

26

paid good fees and the property in Sussex had been sold. Why keep a house when you have no home? Corbett tried to clear the depression from his mind as he left the Palace of Westminster. An hour candle fixed in an iron socket on one of the benches of the court told him it was three in the afternoon. The crowds were dispersing. The litigants with their pile of documents, lawyers elated or depressed, the serjeants, in their multicoloured robes, led lines of prisoners chained together out of the courts to be marched under guard to the Tun, Marshalsea or Newgate Prison.

Corbett threaded his way through them all out of the palace and down to the river bank. He decided to brave the weather and hired a wherry sculled by the ugliest boatman Corbett had ever seen, who insisted on regaling him with the finer parts of his visit to the stews of the city the night before. Eventually, damp and cold, his ears ringing with the waterman's vivid description of his sex life, Hugh reached Queenshithe Wharf and made his way up towards St. Pauls. It was already dark. The last desperate tradesmen, eel-sellers and water carriers, were trying to squeeze as much trade as possible out of the day. The streets were emptying. Children pulled indoors, apprentices putting up the boards and setting out the horn lanterns, as ordered by the City Fathers to give some poor light to the streets at night.

Corbett felt a gloom over the city and recalled Burnell's words about old quarrels festering like pus in the streets and alleyways of the city. He bought a penny loaf from a baker's last batch and snatched mouthfuls of it as he walked up Fish Street, picking his way around the puddles and heaps of rubbish, trying to block out the rank smell from the fish stalls. An empty charcoal wagon clattered past, its driver as black as the devil but evidently pleased at a good day's trade. Corbett drew in under the porch of a house to let it pass, noticing that across the street, a solitary figure sat locked by the hands in the stocks, a rotten fish dangling round his neck. Some crafty fishmonger, Corbett thought, caught by his own guild or the ever inquisitive city authorities for selling bad produce and so sentenced to public ridicule.

Corbett walked on and turned into Cheapside, a broad avenue which cut east to west across the city and the focal point of London's trade. The houses were bigger and grander here. Two or three storeys high, with windows glazed with horn, the wattled daub clean and the timbers and gables brightly painted, most of them displaying the arms of the Guild of Goldsmiths. At one of these houses, Corbett stopped and knocked at the heavy wooden door. There was a rattle of chains and locks and the door swung slightly open on its thick stout leather hinges. A burly porter, carrying a cresset torch of spluttering pitch, brusquely asked Corbett's business. The clerk curbed his anger at the man's rudeness and asked to speak with the merchant, John de Guisars. The porter was set to slam the door in Corbett's face when a small, rotund figure appeared, standing on tiptoe to see him.

"Why," he exclaimed, almost pushing his retainer aside. "It is Hugh Corbett. Come to deposit more monies, Master Clerk?"

Hugh grinned at the fat, generous face. He had always liked de Guisars, who made little attempt to hide his acquisitiveness.

"No, Master Goldsmith," he replied. "I have come to check your stewardship and draw monies from you." The goldsmith's disappointment was almost laughable. He regarded Corbett as a good customer who always deposited money and rarely drew on his stock. A mysterious man really, the goldsmith thought, looking at the clerk's dark, gaunt face and hooded eyes. The clerk was quite wealthy but lived sparsely in some garret in Thames Street.

The goldsmith's shrewd little eyes saw a mystery in the man but he was too polite to ever comment. He sighed, beckoned the clerk into the blackness of the inner shop and ordered the now submissive doorkeeper to light candles and bring his visitor some wine. De Guisars led Corbett by the arm deeper into the house and bade him sit on a small stool. The doorkeeper, taper in hand, lit the tallow and wax candles which stood in iron holders placed judiciously around a room which exuded wealth and comfort. The floor was polished wood, thick, gilt-edged tapestries depicting richly woven scenes from the Bible covered the walls. At the far end was a large oak table, a chair and, above them, racks and shelves full of scrolls or sheaves of parchment all neatly ordered and indexed. On each side of the table were leather and wooden chests reinforced with iron strips and heavily padlocked. The wine was eventually brought, two cups of what Corbett recognized as the best of Gascony, warmed and lightly spiced. He and de Guisars toasted each other and, when the porter withdrew, the goldsmith sat on a trunk opposite Corbett.

"How much?" he asked.

Corbett smiled. "Ten pounds but don't worry, Master de Guisars, most of it will come back. It's the King's business."

The goldsmith nodded in pleasure. With the cup clasped between his hands he looked like some ancient child. "And the business?" he asked hopefully.

Corbett knew that de Guisars would ask that question and had carefully planned his response. "Well," he answered slowly. "Yes, I can tell you. It's Duket. A member of your guild who hanged himself in Saint Mary Le Bow. I have been asked to investigate ... " His voice trailed off as he noticed de Guisars's reaction. Fear? Terror? Even guilt? Corbett could not decide but the transformation in the little merchant was astonishing. His face went white and he became visibly flustered.

De Guisars rose swiftly from his seat and crossed to one of his leather trunks. Within minutes he had counted out Corbett's money and, crossing over, almost threw it into Corbett's hand as if anxious to be rid of him. "Your money, Master Clerk." He opened the door. "It is late and ... " he waved airily towards the back of his house.

Corbett rose, slid the coins into his purse and moved towards the open door. "Goodnight, Master de Guisars," he murmured. "Perhaps I will be back."

In the cold, dark street, Corbett heard the door slam behind him, aware that already his commission had stirred troubled waters. He looked up through the narrow gaps between the projecting houses. The sky was clear, the stars distant and very bright. Corbett knew that the night would be freezing cold and began to walk briskly down the almost deserted Cheapside. He saw shadows move in an alleyway so he drew the long dagger from beneath his cloak and the shadows receded into the darkness. Corbett stopped outside a tavern, its long ale stake and the warmth and light beckoning him in. He was cold and hungry, and he suddenly realized how little he had eaten that day, but he looked down Cheapside to the dark mass of St. Mary Le Bow and regretfully decided that the tavern would have to wait.

The church of St. Mary Le Bow stood in its own ground, behind a low stone wall, a little removed from the main thoroughfare of Cheapside. The chancel, broad and sheer, faced the street, its square tower and entrance at the far end behind which lay the cemetery whilst alongside and parallel to the church was what Corbett took to be the clergy house, a half-timbered building, with a thatched roof. Both buildings wore an aspect of wear, decay and dilapidation. There was an eerie sadness about the place, a feeling of quiet but baleful menace which curled the hair on the nape of his neck.

Corbett slowly walked round the church. He noted the main entrance in the square tower and a small entrance into the nave which looked as if it had not been used for years. The windows were shuttered and closed, the main door bolted, barred and immovable. He looked up but only the dripping, evil devil-face of a gargoyle stared back. Corbett scuffed the dirt with the toe of his boot and walked over to the clergy house. It looked deserted but, after hammering on the door, he heard the patter of footsteps and the rattle of a bolt being drawn back.

"Who is it?" The voice was harsh but tinged with fear.

"Hugh Corbett, royal clerk, sent down by the King to investigate Lawrence Duket's death." The door swung open and a tall, stooped figure carrying a candle drew back to let Corbett enter.

"What is there to investigate?" Corbett looked at the speaker, the thin, emaciated face, glittering eyes, balding head and straggly beard. He immediately disliked this man in his brown, dirty robe but, at the same time, was slightly wary of him.

"I am on the King's business, not yours," Corbett snapped back, pleased to see the man's claw-like hand grip the candle even tighter. "Who are you, anyway?" he continued.

"I am Roger Bellet," the man replied. "Rector and priest of the church of Saint Mary Le Bow." His eyes slid from Corbett like those of a cowed child and he moved to light more candles.

Corbett looked around the hall of a house, a large room with a door at the far end which probably led out to further rooms and offices. He looked up at the fire-blackened beams and moved nearer a glowing charcoal brazier.

The place repelled him with its dirt-beaten floor and filthy rushes. Corbett was cold, colder in this priestly home than he had been outside. Bellet pulled a stool across for him and offered wine but Corbett refused. He did not trust the man, instead he stretched out his hands to the warmth and waited for the priest to seat himself at the other side of the brazier.

"How can I help you, Master Clerk?" The voice was now ingratiary, the priest's lips stretched in a false smile, showing a row of jagged yellow stumps.

"All you know about Lawrence Duket." Bellet gazed into the glowing heat.

"Very little," he replied. "On the afternoon of thirteenth January, Lawrence Duket stabbed another merchant, Ralph Crepyn, in Cheapside. He fled to this church seeking sanctuary. Of course, I gave it, the man was confused, exhausted and frightened. I gave him wine, some bread and left him in the sanctuary. I locked the door on the outside, he bolted it from within, and a watch from the local ward mounted a guard. The next morning about Prime, just after dawn, I went back into the church and found that Duket had moved the sanctuary chair over to the window embrasure and hanged himself from an iron bar. I and the watch ward immediately cut the body down and sent for the local coroner who called in witnesses and delivered judgement. The rest you must know."

Corbett nodded. "Did you lock the church that night? I mean immediately after you left Duket?"

"No, I came back later. Duket was asleep in the chair, only then did I bolt it for the night." Bellet replied.

"Where did Duket get the rope to hang himself?"

Bellet shrugged. "There is rope in the church," he answered. "Old rope, new rope. It is constantly being used in the belfry. Duket must have found some and carried out his terrible self-destruction."

"The belfry is in the tower?" Corbett asked. "At the far end of the church away from the sanctuary?"

Bellet nodded.

"And Duket?" Corbett continued. "What did he have with him?"

The priest bit his lower lip and leaned back on his stool as if the question really puzzled him. "Not much," he murmured. "The clothes he fled in, his knife and a purse with some money. Why?"

"Nothing," Corbett smiled back. "Nothing. I simply wondered. Where is the body?" he asked. The priest stared at him.

"Duket's body! Where is it?" he demanded again.

The priest shrugged. "Duket was a suicide and was treated as such. The under-sheriff of the city had the body dragged by the heels on a sheet of ox-hide to a place outside the walls and it was buried in the city ditch. The usual fate for anyone who commits such an act."

"No one," Corbett interjected. "No one pleaded for the body?"

"Master Clerk," Bellet replied, staring at him fixedly across the glowing coals. "Duket was a suicide and the church's teaching on that subject is not a matter for debate!"

Corbett pursed his lips and tried to look baffled about the whole affair. "Can I see inside the church?" The priest pointed out that it was dark and little could be seen. Corbett nodded understandably and promised to return the following day. He then took his leave, glad to be out of that room with its shadowy menace and away from a church which offered little comfort to either the dead or the living.

Corbett wandered back to the tavern that he had passed earlier in the evening and entered its warmth and light. He sat at a trestle table and drank some beefy broth generously garnished with leeks and garlic, as well as a quart of heady ale. He felt warm, relaxed and decided he could not face the journey home so he hired a blanket from the landlord and a space to sleep on the rush-strewn floor. He lay down exhausted but unable to forget that dark church with its sinister priest. Vague memories stirred about stories he had heard or read about St. Mary Le Bow. An unhappy building. But why? Where had he learnt that? His tired brain groped for an answer when he suddenly remembered something disturbing. The priest had expected him, almost as if the King always ordered a high-ranking clerk to investigate every suicide in the city. Corbett was still puzzling about that as he fell into a deep sleep.

Four

The next morning Corbett was awakened by one of the tavern slatterns. He felt drowsy and thick-headed after the previous evening. He warmed himself at one of the cooking fires whilst he consumed a breakfast of ale and coarse rye bread. He then picked up his belongings and made his way down Cheapside, calling into the open-fronted stall of a barber who shaved his upper lip and chin with consummate skill and, at Corbett's gentle questioning, supplied details about the local coroner who carried out the inquest on Lawrence Duket. He was a physician, Roger Padgett, who plied his trade in one of the side alleyways off Cheapside. After he left the barber's stall, Corbett found the house, a modest two-timbered affair with the huge gilt sign of a bowl and pestle hanging over the door.

Padgett was a garrulous little man inflated with his own self-importance as a doctor and a coroner. A small pretentious figure in his scarlet cloak slashed with blue and lined with taffeta, who carefully inspected Corbett's warrant before inviting him into the lower room of his house which served as his surgery. Corbett did not trust doctors and saw their secret arts as trickery. He looked around the room and supposed Padgett was no different. There was a Zodiac map on the floor, and along the walls shelves full of clay jars and clearly marked 'senna', 'henbane', 'foxglove' or 'eel skin'. A huge wooden bowl stood on the table, full of a fine white dust which made him sneeze and cough until the physician covered it with a damp cloth.

Padgett sat himself on the room's one and only chair and, ignoring Corbett's comfort, abruptly asked. "How can I be of assistance, Master Clerk?"

"By telling me about Lawrence Duket, how and where did you find the body?"

The physician slouched in his chair, his fingers clutching the arms while he looked above Corbett's head and talked as if he was reciting a poem. "Lawrence Duket was found hanged in the church of Saint Mary Le Bow shortly after daybreak on fourteenth January. I believe the Rector, the priest Bellet, found the body." He looked direct at Corbett. "You have met him?" Corbett nodded and Padgett gave him an odd look before continuing:

"Anyway, Bellet cut the body down, and left it lying in the sanctuary. I and a group of witnesses came to inspect the corpse. There were no marks of violence upon it, no rupture of the skin or any other sign of attack. The only wound was a purple red gash round the neck and a large bruise under the right ear, both of these were caused by the noose and knot of the rope that Duket tied round his throat when he hanged himself. I then investigated the place of death. A large metal bar which juts out from the side of one of the windows in the sanctuary and the Blessed Chair had been pushed under it. Duket apparently used this to stand on, tied the halter around the bar, fastened the noose about his neck and then simply stepped off the chair. The only extraordinary thing were these black silk threads found around the noose." He handed them over to Corbett, who studied them for a while before slipping them into his own wallet.

The physician then looked at Corbett and grimaced with his small prim mouth. "That is all. There were the usual signs of a hanged person. The bowels and stomach had emptied, the face had turned a blueish-purple, the tongue was swollen and bitten and the eyes protuberant."

"Nothing else? No sign whatsoever of any violence?" Corbett impatiently interrupted him.

"It was," Padgett said slowly, "as I have described for you. I think that Duket killed Crepyn, fled to the church and, through fear or remorse, hanged himself."

"There were no other signs, no marks on the body?" Corbett persisted and raised a hand to placate the physician's evident annoyance, before continuing: "Of course, your report was very complete. The Lord Chancellor himself commented on that but, was there anything that your professional eye noted but dismissed as having nothing to do with the death?"

"Only one thing," came the quick smug reply. "Duket had bruises on the upper arms but they were probably only bruises, nothing else."

Corbett smiled. "Thank you, Master Padgett, and if you remember anything please send it to the chancery." Before the bemused physician could answer, Corbett was through the door striding up the street back towards Cheapside.

A pale sun had broken through a cloudy sky drawing the usual crowds into Cheapside. Scriveners with their portable trays were ready for business. The stalls were up, the shop fronts down and business was very brisk. There were merchants in Flemish beaver hats and leather boots, lawyers with scrolls under their arms, apprentices in surcoats and hose, women of all kinds and every profession. Haughty ladies in their heavy folded dresses, girdled by low-slung, jewelled belts, their heads adorned with linen wimples and their soft bodies protected by their fur-lined cloaks.

The noise and clamour of the street were all the more strident to Corbett, so used to the quiet serenity of the chancery. Merchants and drapers tried to interest him in velvet, silks or lawn. Food stall-owners and bakers offered hot spiced ribs of beef, eel and meat pies garnished with leeks and onions. Two stall-holders fought over a pile of pewter pots. Corbett saw two pockets picked and held his own purse tightly under his cloak, ever vigilant against the legion of thieves in the capital. A string of hapless, convicted felons were led through the crowd by a group of constables taking them from the Tun to Newgate, and these unfortunates were subject to every abuse possible by those who considered themselves lucky not to be one of them. There were two bawds, naked except for their petticoats, doing penance though their bold eyes, saucy looks, as well as the lewd sniggers of some of the spectators, made it obvious they would soon be back at their trade.

At one time the press of people was so great that Corbett panicked for a while, remembering that fatal press of bodies before the royal pavilion in Wales so many years before. The moment, however, passed and he was through, standing once more before the gate leading to Saint Mary Le Bow. Once again he sensed that feeling of desolation and dread that he had experienced before and tried to remember what he knew about the church but the memory escaped him. The place was deserted except for a few gawking onlookers who promptly disappeared as the black-gowned figure of Bellet strode across to meet Corbett. "Ah, Master Clerk," the priest proffered a bony hand which Corbett clasped, aware that the priest's white gaunt features and sombre dress only enhanced the sinister fear he had experienced on the previous night.

"I have come to view the church," Corbett announced more abruptly than he had intended. "Now, in the light of day."

"All will be revealed!" the priest quietly retorted and

Corbett thought Bellet was more confident than he had sounded the night before but he only nodded his assent and allowed Bellet to escort him up to the main door in the church.

Inside, the entrance was dark and smelt of must and damp. Corbett stopped and looked around, his attention was caught by a narrow iron-studded door on his left. He ignored all else and moved across to open it. "It's locked," Bellet smugly commented. "It has been for months. It leads up to the belfry and the tower roof but, if you want ... " His voice trailed off as if he was bored.

"Yes," Corbett replied testily, "I want. Open it!"

The priest, his lips pursed in a half-smile, fumbled with a heavy bunch of keys which swung from his belt and eventually he unlocked the door. It creaked open, protesting loudly on its rusty hinges. Corbett brushed past the priest and began to climb the wet, mildewed spiral staircase. The belfry was at the top, its great bronze bells now hanging silent. Corbett gave them a cursory glance and, pulling back the heavy iron bolts, began to push and heave at the thick wooden trapdoor above him until it began to creak and lift upwards.

The wind whipped Corbett's face as he emerged from the trapdoor and stood on the tower roof. He approached the short crenellated wall and stared down to where Cheapside lay dizzily small beneath him. The city stretched out on either side, a row of roofs and houses to the south and the brown soil and snow-covered fields to the north beyond Newgate and the old city wall. Corbett looked round the tower. Someone could have lurked there and made their way down into the church itself but the trapdoor, as well as the door to the tower, looked as if they had not been used for years and any intruder who used them would have roused Duket, the ward watch and half of Cheapside.

Corbett shook his head and made his way down to where the priest was waiting for him, a sardonic grin on his sallow features.

"Did you find anything, Master Clerk?" Corbett ignored the sarcasm in his voice and stared round the porch. In one corner, bell ropes dangled down from a small aperture in the ceiling; beneath them, coiled in rough heaps, were other pieces of rope. Some of them new, some old and frayed.

"This was where Duket took the rope from?"

The priest nodded. "Yes," he replied, "he must have come down here to collect the rope and then gone back to the sanctuary."

"In the dark?" Corbett asked.

"What do you mean?" was the surly reply.

"I mean," Corbett said slowly, "that Duket sat here in the sanctuary in the dark and then quietly made his way down into the gloom to collect a piece of rope to kill himself?"

"He had a candle," the priest answered quickly.

"If he did," Corbett commented, waving his hand round the porch, "then he did not use it. There is no trace of fresh wax on the floor!" He looked at Bellet, pleased to see the sardonic grin disappear from his face. "An agitated man," Corbett continued, "carrying a candle, stumbling around in the dark. His hand would shake." Corbett scuffed the floor with the toe of his boot. "There would be more wax here than dirt!"

Corbett turned and walked into the nave of the church, a large paved area which stretched down to the rood screen, a wooden trellised partition with a huge door in the centre which led into the sanctuary and the stairs to the high altar. There was a row of stout squat pillars down either side of the nave. Each of the transepts looked black and empty except for the stacked wooden benches and the faded frescoes on the dirty whitewashed walls. High above each transept was a row of small oval-shaped windows. Corbett stared up at them, they were all firmly shuttered both inside and out except for one where the shutters hung loose, though still too small for any man to get through unnoticed by either Duket or the ward watch.

Corbett pulled his cloak around him and walked further down the nave, noting even how his leather-soled boots echoed like drumbeats round the church. He could hear the priest slithering behind him like some rat creeping along a pipe. Corbett walked into the sanctuary. The Blessed Chair, thick heavy and wooden, sat like a throne at the bottom of the white stone altar. There was nothing to see, though Corbett realized that he had never been in such a stark, lonely sanctuary. The high altar rose above him, lonely and impassive, its marble ledge unadorned by flowers or linen cloths. Behind it was a reredos, a blank screen with a faded fresco and above it a lonely red sanctuary lamp gleamed and winked in the gloom. There were benches at either side. Corbett turned and looked up, there was a trefoil window meshed with wire and horn above the high altar, which provided most of the light, flanked by a row of shuttered windows as in the rest of the church.

He walked over to the right of the sanctuary and looked up at the iron bar jutting out beside the large, wooden shuttered window. "Is that the bar?"

The priest, standing behind him, one hand on the arm of the Blessed Chair, nodded. "Yes," he replied slowly. "The chair had been moved by Duket. He must have used it to fasten the rope round the bar."

Corbett turned, looked directly at Bellet and shook his head. "I would not be too sure about that," he replied and, not waiting for a reply, walked back down the nave of the church.

Corbett left the church and turned into the area below

Friday Street occupied by foreign tanners. The place was now a scene of frenetic building activity as workmen were engaged in constructing a huge cistern or conduit which would hold water run through elm pipes from the Tyburn Stream. It was also the gallows ground and two bodies, fresh carrion by the look of them, hung twirling by their necks from the crude crossbeam of the scaffold. At any other time Corbett would have quickly passed such a scene but now, with the image of Lawrence Duket hanging by his neck at Saint Mary Le Bow fresh in his mind, Corbett went up and closely studied the bodies. Impervious to the smell and the horror of the grisly corpses, Corbett stayed till he was satisfied and then moved away to ask the whereabouts of Duket's house. His enquiries usually drew dark looks or blank stares but at last he was directed to a house on the corner of Bread Street.

A modest, two-storeyed building, Corbett thought it was deserted for the front door was secured tightly as were all the shutters. Corbett, however, pounded on the door, shouting for it to be opened "on the King's business". He heard footsteps, the bolts drawn and the door was opened by a small slim woman of medium height with auburn hair caught up in a wimple, the air of sobriety and mourning completed by a long, black dress. The only concession to fashion was a filigree gold chain round her waist and fresh white lace round the cuffs and long slim neck. Her face was severe with petulant lips and arrogant grey eyes. Corbett offered his warrant, the woman took it and read it quietly, her lips moving slowly over the words, she returned it and beckoned Corbett into the lower room, opening the shutters to allow in some air and light. The place was bereft of furniture except for leather trunks and heaps of clothing.

The woman watched Corbett for a while. "I am Jean Duket," she said softly. "What do you want with me?" The words had a faint suggestive tone which Corbett ignored as he described his interest in Lawrence Duket's death. Although the woman was in mourning weeds, she seemed little disturbed by her brother's death. Only when Corbett mentioned Crepyn's name did Jean's eyes narrow, the colour rising in her cheeks.

"I did not like Crepyn, Master Clerk," she snapped. "He was," she searched for words.

"A blackmailer?" Corbett prompted her.

"Yes, Master Corbett, a blackmailer, a nothing, a fornicator and despoiler of women!"

"So, the story is true?" Corbett queried. Jean did not answer but turned and nodded her head vigorously.

"Is that why Lawrence killed him?" Corbett persisted.

Jean turned and laughed, almost hysterical. "Master Clerk, my brother and I, though we shared the same womb and later the same house, did not love each other." She laughed nervously. "My brother did not kill for me. There were other things!" She looked quickly at Corbett. "I do not know, but the Bitch will know!"

"Who is this Bitch, Madam?"

"Alice atte Bowe, she keeps a tavern in St. Mark's Lane, the haunt of others of her coven or company. Reginald de Lanfer, Robert Pinnot, Paul Stubberhead, Thomas Coroner ...?" Her voice trailed off and she stood twisting her waist chain in her fingers. "She was Crepyn's mistress. An evil whore!" She almost spat the words out of her mouth. "Crepyn forced me to sleep with him, to strip and pose, and then he told her and others what had happened." Jean slumped on to one of the trunks, her head in her hands.

Corbett just stood and watched for a while. "Was Lawrence Alice's lover as well?" he asked.

Jean lifted her head back and laughed loudly. "My brother, Master Clerk, did not like women. As to the real cause of his quarrel with Crepyn," she looked directly at Corbett. "I do not know, I do not care and, in days, I will be free of here. I have relatives in Oxford. I shall go there." She rose and smoothed the folds of her dress. "That is all, Master Corbett. I wish you well." She opened the door and stood aside to let Corbett pass through into the street.

Outside Corbett suddenly felt tired and hungry and eager for his own bed. He bought a pie from a nearby stall and ate it as he walked, quite determined to stay away from the taverns and their heady drink, at least for one night. He had begun his task as a good clerk should by collecting facts and information and, now was trying to organize it into some recognizable pattern. Yet there were items which confused and perplexed him and he knew his chancery-trained mind would give him no rest until everything was in order.

He turned off Cheapside down Paternoster Row and eventually arrived outside his lodgings in Thames Street just as darkness fell. He entered the house, ordered a lighted brazier from the owner, the sulky wife of a merchant, and climbed the rickety stairs to his garret. For a while he lay on his bed, swathed in his cloak as he recalled all he had seen, heard or said. Gradually, a pattern began to emerge in his mind and, having lit candles, he undid his bundle and, picking out his writing tray, slowly began to write on a piece of used parchment the facts now so clear in his mind.

Five

Corbett slept late that morning and, when he awoke, returned to the document he had drawn up the previous evening, studying it carefully and making corrections until he was satisfied. He then washed, dressed and, after a quick meal, took his cloak and left his lodgings to walk briskly towards the river. A bright winter sun seemed to add to his mood of quiet expectancy about his mission. He was quite confident about what had happened in the church of Saint Mary Le Bow, though he was baffled as to why and how. These questions perplexed him throughout his short walk to the east Watergate where he hired a boat to take him to Westminster. The journey was cold, quick and noisome. At Westminster he disembarked, pulled the hood of his cloak over his head to avoid recognition and pushed through the crowds, taking a path around the Great Hall to the buildings beyond. Here he went towards one of the small outbuildings, knocked on the door and demanded entrance. When a querulous voice told him to go away, he knocked again and eventually the door swung open to reveal a tall, ascetic man dressed in a long brown robe. His face was pale, long and lined, and his watery eyes squinted at the daylight. "Master Couville. It is I, Hugh Corbett. Are you so blind you cannot see me or just so senile you cannot recognize me?" The old man's drawn face broke into a smile and thin blue-veined hands clasped Corbett by the arms.

"Only you, Hugh, would dare insult me," he murmured. "My best pupil! Come in. Come in. It's cold outside."

Hugh entered the room, the light was poor and the air was musty with the smell of tallow, charcoal and the lingering perfume of leather and old parchment. There was a trestle table and a huge stool, the rest of the room being taken up with leather and wooden chests of all sizes. Some were open with rolls of parchment spilling out onto the floor; around the walls on shelves stretching up to the blackened ceiling were more rolls of parchment. It all looked very disorganized but Corbett knew that Couville could accurately pick out any manuscript he wanted. This was part of the records office of the Chancery and Exchequer dating back centuries. If a document was issued or received, it would be filed in the appropriate place and this was Nigel Couville's kingdom. Once a principal clerk in the Chancery, he had been given this assignment as a benefice or sinecure, a reward for long faithful service to the Crown. Couville had been Corbett's master and mentor when Hugh first became a clerk and, despite the gap of years and experience, they became close friends.

There were questions, comments, but Corbett deftly fended off the old man's solicitous enquiries until Couville laughed. "Come, Hugh," he asked. "What do you want? You're here for a purpose besides teasing an old man?" Corbett grinned, nodded and described his mission as quickly as he could and detailed what he was looking for. The old man sat and listened patiently. When Corbett finished, Couville rose and, one hand covering his mouth, stared around the room, his eyes flickering from one chest to another. He shook his head. "I am sorry, Hugh. I cannot help you here. What you are looking for will be in one of the depository rooms at the Tower." Corbett's heart sank at the prospect of another long journey and days, even weeks, searching through the thousands of records at the Tower under the watchful if obstructive eye of some strange clerk. Couville sensed the young man's bitter disappointment. He put one scrawny hand on his young friend's shoulder. "Do not worry, Hugh. I will get what you want. I still have some authority. It may take a day or even two but I will get it and send it to you."

Corbett embraced the old man. "Thank you," he said. "That will at least be part reparation for being such a hard taskmaster!" He turned and left with the old man shouting affectionate abuse and insisting that Corbett's next visit be longer.

Corbett, however, was already striding through the mud, muffled and hooded, slightly disappointed with his visit to Couville but determined to get to St. Mark's Lane and the tavern of Alice atte Bowe. He knew the area well, a small lane off Paternoster Row near the Cathedral Church of St. Paul's. Corbett walked some of the way but then hitched a lift from a carter on Fleet Street who was taking produce in from the country to the stalls and markets of the city. Along Paternoster Row, Corbett left the carter and went down Ivy Lane into the square bounded by the monastery of Greyfriars at one end and the soaring church of St. Paul's at another. There were more stalls and shops here and, though late afternoon, it was still very busy. Corbett, however, was cautious, securing his purse and keeping his hand on his dagger as he passed through the great west gate into the church of St. Paul's. The area was a well-known haunt of 'Wolfsheads', outlaws and members of the city's murky underworld, who lived in and around the church ready to bolt for sanctuary should the forces of the law appear.

Corbett walked through the main door of St. Paul's into the main meeting place under its vaulting nave. It was still busy. At the west end sat twelve scribes ready to prepare documents, indentures, letters, bonds for anyone willing to hire their services. Serjeants-at-law in their ermine-lined robes stood in the aisles, meeting clients or discussing the finer points of law with each other, while around one pillar, anxious serving-men waited to be hired. Corbett searched about until he saw the person he was looking for, a scrivener with his writing trays seated on a stool in a small alcove. He looked almost like a human bird, fine small claw-like hands and a small round head tilted to one side with a cheerful ruddy face under a shock of white hair. Corbett walked over.

"Matthew!" he called out. "How's business?"

The scribe looked up, spread his hands and shrugged. "Fair, it comes and goes. But what can I do for you?"

"Alice atte Bowe," Corbett replied. "She owns a tavern in St. Mark's Lane. Which one and what do you know of her?"

Corbett knew that Matthew was an incorrigible gossip with a genius for picking up the scandal of the city. He was surprised to see the man's eyes flicker sideways and the fear emanate from him like a perfume. Matthew looked nervously around and beckoned Corbett to crouch beside him.

"Is this about Crepyn's death and Duket's suicide at Saint Mary Le Bow?" he asked. Corbett nodded and Matthew bit his lower lip nervously.

"Be careful," he whispered. "They say that Alice is a dangerous woman. She was, according to common report, Crepyn's mistress. She has connections with the powerful Lanfor family. She married a vintner, Thomas atte Bowe, an old man who died soon after the marriage leaving her the family business. The tavern she owns is called 'The Mitre'. It is a large place. It is also a dangerous one. Now, please go."

Corbett obeyed the scribe, surprised at his reaction and concerned that this gregarious scrivener should be frightened of a mere name.

Corbett found 'The Mitre' tavern in St. Mark's Lane, an elaborate two-storeyed affair with the upper floor jutting out over the central door. A large ale stake, and the sign of a bishop's mitre against a black background, made it the most obvious building in the street. As he entered, Corbett noted the bishop's face on the sign was a mocking caricature of a churchman, pompous, cruel and greedy. Inside, it was dark but comfortable, much cleaner than many such establishments. A long room with whitewashed walls, clean rushes on the floor sprinkled with crushed herbs. The ceiling was quite high with timbered rafters black from the hearth in the centre of the room with a flue above it to allow the smoke to escape. Along the walls there were stools, rough benches and trestle tables.

A huge, bald-headed man stood before the hearth, his small piggy eyes scrutinized Corbett before sliding away to look at the customers scattered round the room. There were the usual drunks, fast asleep at the tables, a few solitary individuals totally involved in their own thoughts or cups and a group of men lazily tossing dice watched by a bawd in a scarlet gown and head-dress. Pot-boys and drawers served the groups, both with wine and ale under the severe scrutiny of the bald-headed giant. No one else noticed Corbett's entrance except for a small group of men in the far corner who studied him for a while and then turned back to their own conversation.

Corbett sat at one table and ordered wine and food from one of the tapsters. He ate his meal slowly while he took in his surroundings. Somehow he was aware that he was recognized, almost expected, and that what he was seeing was a tableau, something staged for his own benefit. After a while Corbett beckoned the huge bald-headed man over to his table. The man saw his gesture but studiously ignored him for a time and then, after biting his nail and spitting into the fire, moved across to him.

"Sir?" The voice was rather high for such a big man.

"My name is Hugh Corbett, clerk in the King's Bench. I am here on the King's business. I have a warrant which proves this and I would like to speak to Mistress Alice atte Bowe."

His words like stones thrown into a pool spread ripples, circles of silence around the tavern. The conversation dropped to a low hum, the dice rolled, heads did not turn but he was aware of ears straining to hear him. The large man simply looked at him with his small pebble-black eyes and then, beckoning to Corbett, turned and walked to the far end of the tavern. Corbett followed him into a second room at the back which served as a kitchen. A small whitewashed place with a long table covered in pewter and earthenware pots. At the far end was a fire with a roast on a spit and, above it, a row of iron flesh hooks.

The place was clean and smelt of the crushed herbs and spices which were packed in pots on shelves around the room. At the far end of the table, almost unnoticed, was the small, slim figure of a woman studying a piece of parchment. At Corbett's entrance, she looked up and slipped the parchment beneath the table. Corbett had never seen such beauty, a Flemish white-laced head-dress framed a small olive face, large dark eyes, perfectly chiselled nose and lips which would have tempted the holiest hermit. A lock of black hair had escaped from under her head-dress to lie on a perfect cheek. She was small, petite, but the green gown and gold waist belt emphasized, not hid her beautiful body with its swelling breasts and slim waist. Corbett could only stare as the giant introduced him. The woman gazed at him with eyes full of laughter and a smile which showed her perfect teeth as well as her pleasure at meeting him.

"So, Master Corbett, what can we do for you?" The voice

was low and surprisingly deep. Corbett thought she was laughing at him and could only stand and shuffle his feet like some country bumpkin. The woman turned to the giant still standing threateningly close to Corbett. "Peter," she said. "You can go. I do not think that Master Corbett is here to arrest me. I think I am perfectly safe though I suspect that Master Corbett may not feel so secure!"

Her gentle mockery jolted Corbett into some form of self-assurance. "Madam," he said, "I am here to ask you a few questions. I am here on the King's commission!" He looked at the mocking laughter in her eyes and his voice trailed off into silence.

Alice beckoned to a place near her on one of the benches which ran the length of the huge table. He sat, aware that Peter the giant was being silently dismissed back into the front room of the tavern. Corbett looked at the fine-grained table top. He felt shy and tongue-tied, wanting to gaze again into those wide dark eyes. He was drawn to this woman like a deer, hunted and thirsty, is drawn to a clear babbling spring of water. He heard the retreating giant's footsteps and looked up. Her eyes were not dark, he realized but a deep blue, surrounded by laughter lines.

"Mistress Alice," he blurted out. "What do you know about the death of Lawrence Duket?"

Alice stared at him, lips pursed deep in thought. "What should I know, Master Clerk?" she replied. "I can guess you know that I knew both Duket and Crepyn. But I had nothing to do with the deaths of either man."

Corbett could feel the cool, calm superiority of the woman and decided to reassert himself in a mood of official brusqueness. After all, who was this woman but a tavern-keeper? "Mistress Bowe," he snapped, "common report has it that you were Crepyn's mistress and that the fatal quarrel between him and Duket was caused by you."

Mistress Bowe simply stared at Corbett, then broke into peals of laughter which burst out like pearls cascading from a chest. "Master Corbett, I was Crepyn's friend but not his mistress and Duket certainly did not like me or any woman."

Her words jolted Corbett back to reality. He remembered similar words on the lips of Jean Duket. Alice, studiously watching him, seemed to sense his mood and the danger of this inquisitive man breaking free of the spell she had so cleverly spun. She placed one lace-framed hand on Corbett's wrist and only then did he notice that both her hands were covered in soft, fine, black silk gloves. She noticed his curiosity and laughed. "Master Corbett, do not be surprised. I am a lady and these gloves protect my hands. A lady's hands should be as soft and smooth as shot-silk. Should they not?"

Corbett nodded. "Nevertheless Madam," he replied without thinking, "like the truth they should be seen." He could feel her hand on his as if it was a hot, glowing coal searing into his flesh. Suddenly, he felt afraid, like a swimmer out of his depth who wanted to give way to a strong current and be carried wherever it wished.

He abruptly removed her hand. "Madam, do you know anything about the deaths of either man?"

She bent her head and smoothed the polished top of the table with her gloved hands. "Of course I did," she replied in a matter-of-fact tone of voice. "Both men supped and drank here many times. I was friendly with both, lover to neither."

"Why did you say Duket was never attracted to women?" Corbett continued.

She shrugged. "He was like that," she replied. "He never complimented me, unlike other men, and I never saw him with a woman."

"Was he a sodomite?" Corbett asked.

"No, Master Corbett. I think not. Why, are you?" The pert question angered him and he felt the blood surge from his heart and the heat enter his cheeks and eyes.

"Madam," he snapped. "You forget yourself!"

"Sir," she replied, her eyes now bright and brittle with temper. "You come into my house and suggest that I am a whore, the mistress of one man and the possible cause of the death of two. It is you, sir, who forget yourself!"

Corbett rose, the bench falling behind him with a crash. "Madam," he bowed and turned to go but she too rose, her eyes now pleading, a soft hand on his arm.

"Master Clerk," she said softly. "I am sorry!"

Corbett turned to pick up the fallen bench, he stumbled, hit his back on the table and almost fell. He turned, face flushed, and noticed she was now stifling the laughter. He grinned, shuffled his feet, picked up the bench and sat down again. The giant, Peter, reappeared, drawn by the crash of the bench and the raised voices, but Alice dismissed him with a wave of her gloved hand and, touching Corbett lightly on the shoulder, moved to another part of the kitchen and brought back two brimming goblets of wine. "The best Bordeaux," she said. "Please. Drink. I'm sorry I offended you."

Corbett toasted her with his cup and drank slowly. The wine was good, its sweetness filling his mouth and throat while he listened to her speak. She described her marriage, widowhood, the management of the tavern and the nature of her relationship with the two dead men. "I knew both men," she repeated, "but only because they came here."

"Jean Duket called you a whore and Crepyn's mistress," Corbett replied. "Why?"

She grinned. "Jean was a stupid, malicious woman with a tongue like the clapper of a bell. She can say what she likes but her words are the fruit of anger and envy."

"Do you know why Crepyn and Duket argued?" Corbett enquired.

"No, I do not."

"Or why Duket should commit suicide?"

"No," Alice replied. "But he was always a timid man. Fearful of his own shadow!"

"What was Crepyn involved in?"

Alice sat and thought, the doubt and perplexity visible in her beautiful eyes and face. "He was a money-lender," she replied slowly. "A man who rose high in city politics. A man of the Populares who was loyal enough to the Crown but still supported the radical politics of the great ... " she stammered, "of de Montfort."

"And Duket? Why did he quarrel with Crepyn?"

"Crepyn was a money-lender disliked by many people. The Dukets were not the only ones caught in his net."

She lowered her eyes. "Perhaps Crepyn deserved what he got," she continued softly. "Sometimes I used to warn him but he only laughed." There was a silence as she played with the hem of one of her silk gloves.

"Is that all?" Corbett asked.

She nodded. "For a while," she added, then rose and walked to a large chest in the far corner of the kitchen. She took out a flute and brought it back to Corbett. "Your visit has saddened me, Master Clerk. I feel unhappy and angry at the stupid deaths of two men I knew. I always find the flute soothes the roused humours of both mind and body."

Corbett sat as if in a trance. The flute was almost the replica of one he had owned in the golden time so long ago. Before it disappeared in a funeral pyre on which he had thrown the shattered flute. He stretched out his hand like a dreamer and took the flute, stroking its polished wood as if it was the face of a long-lost child who had suddenly returned. He put it to his lips and played, the spine-tingling, haunting tune, bitter-sweet, filled the room with its sound. Hugh played and could almost feel the Sussex sun on his face, almost see the small child dance and laugh, while his wife leaned against a wall, arms folded smiling at both player and dancer. He played on, ignoring the hot tears which scalded his eyes and rolled down his face. Then it was gone, both the music and the vision and he was alone in a room with a beautiful woman staring fixedly at him.

Corbett laid the flute down gently on the table, bowed and walked quietly out of the kitchen, through the tavern into the cold darkness of the street. He had forgotten about his mission, for old wounds had been opened and the pus poured out. He saw the dirt and filth of the street and the rubbish-filled gutter. The wine stains along the wall, the mongrel dog sniffing at the bloated body of a dead rat, the beggar in rags, covered with sores, cowering in the corner from the cold and the world. He knew he should not have played the flute; the world had been ordered then, closed and neatly filed like the scrolls in Couville's record office. In such a world he saw nothing good but, there again, nothing ugly. He felt the nightmares returning and remembered the disordered life he had led after his wife had died and the months he had spent in the cool darkness of that Sussex monastery. Then, just as he was about to leave Paternoster Row, he felt a hand on his elbow. He turned, and recognized one of the tapsters from The Mitre. The lad thrust the flute into Corbett's hands.

"My mistress," he said, "says you should keep it and come again and play for her." Corbett nodded and, gripping the flute, disappeared into the darkness.

Six

Corbett had taken from the coroner the names of the three wardsmen who had mounted guard on Saint Mary Le Bow and, the day after he had met Alice, he decided to interrogate them. All three were tradesmen plying their individual craft in the alleyways and lanes of Cheapside. All three swore to the same story and Corbett felt sure that they were speaking the truth as they saw it; they had been summoned by a messenger from one of the under-sheriffs of the city to guard the entrance of the church late in the afternoon on the same day that Lawrence Duket had fled there for sanctuary. They had assembled just before Vespers, had gone into the entrance of the church and seen Duket sitting in the Blessed Chair fast asleep. They had watched him stir, awake and so they left to stand guard outside.

After the bells of the nearby churches had rung for Vespers, (those of Saint Mary Le Bow did not because of Duket's presence), the rector had come and locked the church. They ensured it was secure and heard Duket push home the inside bolts. The door being safely fastened, they planned their watch according to a rota, one would sleep while two mounted guard. A brazier was lit for warmth in the shelter of some trees and, though all three confessed it was freezing cold and sinister to be in a graveyard on such a wild night, nothing untoward happened. They patrolled the church perimeter, they saw no one approach and found it impossible to conceive of how anyone could, even if he slipped by their guard, enter the church for all entrances a man could use were locked and secure. Thus it remained until dawn when the rector returned. He unlocked the door but could not open it, so he asked the watch to help him force it. They beat upon the door to waken Duket, thinking he was asleep and, when this proved fruitless, forced the door with a log until it bent in and the inside bolts snapped.

They found the church as it had been the previous evening. No marks on the floor or any sign of disturbance except in the sanctuary where the chair had been pushed over to the right-hand corner of the sanctuary near the wall. Above this, swinging from an iron bar fixed near the window, was the black-faced, lifeless body of Lawrence Duket. The rector and the wardsmen immediately ran down the church but one look at the dead man's face made them realize that it was too late. They looked around for any sign of disturbance or forced entry but found none. Bellet told them to stand near the body and guard it while he left to send for the coroner. Corbett knew what happened next and made each of the three men repeat their statements, especially the details about their forced entry through the main door. Corbett knew instinctively that the men were not liars, they had no ties with either Duket or Crepyn though they knew of them. They were three rather baffled tradesmen, who had tried to do their duty only to fail in the most mysterious circumstances, for all three swore that no one got into the church, nor did they hear any sound from it during their entire watch.

Satisfied, Corbett returned to the house of the coroner, where he made his request of a rather surprised and now petulant official. Of course, the coroner was shocked at his request, but when Corbett argued his case and flourished

Burnell's writ, he reluctantly agreed and sent a servant to the
Guildhall with a message. He told Corbett that it would take
some time so Corbett decided to visit the stalls and booths
along Cheapside.

It was late in the afternoon when he returned to the
coroner's house to find two burly individuals carrying
spades and a hoe lounging dejectedly outside the door.
Inside the coroner was mixing some evil-smelling paste and
beside him, looking almost ill with the smell, was a tall,
young man with shoulder-length greasy hair, poxed face
and sallow features. The coroner introduced him as Stephen
Novile, bailiff of the city and, with little ceremony, ushered
both of them to the door. The bailiff seemed relieved to be
going, though wary of Corbett.

"You know what you are doing, Master Clerk?" The voice
was a high treble, almost squeaky.

"Yes," Corbett replied. "I want you and your assistants,"
he turned to nod at the wooden-looking labourers, "to take
me where Duket's body is buried in the city ditch. I am on
the King's business," he continued crisply. "The body
belongs to a suicide and so we are not disturbing hallowed
ground. The coroner sent for all three of you as I
understand that you were responsible for the burial. Yes?"

The bailiff nodded, his thin lips pursed, his shifty watery
eyes unable to hold Corbett's gaze. He snapped his fingers at
the two labourers and all four set off silently up Cheapside,
through the shambles, past Newgate and across the old city
walls.

The bailiff then turned to the right and walked down
Cock Lane, a narrow rutted track with an open sewer
running down the centre. It was an area notorious for its
prostitutes, many of whom stood in the darkened doorways,
their hair dyed and faces heavily painted. Dressed in
eye-catching red and orange, they called out invitations

couched in the lewdest way to every passer-by. One of them evidently recognized the bailiff and, for a short while, ran alongside them giving a graphic description of the man's sexual prowess in bed. The bailiff, his face plum-coloured with anger and embarrassment, squeaked with indignation. Corbett tried to hide his smiles and ignore the evident amusement of the two labourers who would have encouraged the woman even further if the bailiff had not turned and glared at them.

At last, they found themselves before the great city ditch which ran the entire length of the city wall. Twenty feet wide, its true depth unknown, the ditch had served the city as both sewer and cesspit since the days of King John the Angevin. The smell was indescribable and Corbett immediately pulled the hem of his cloak up over his mouth and nose. The ditch was full of refuse frozen hard by the winter cold and Corbett could only guess what it was like in the full heat of summer. The bailiff had come forearmed and he held a wine-soaked rag to his nose though the two labourers seemed oblivious to it all, walking backwards and forwards along the edge of the ditch, talking and mumbling as they tried to locate the actual spot where Duket was buried.

Corbett did not envy them their task, the ditch was full of refuse, already he had seen a rat gnawing and tugging at some mud-encrusted lump. The place was a dumping ground for dead cats, dogs, unwanted babies as well as the corpses of executed criminals and suicides. The labourers finally decided on the spot and began to dig then, cursing each other, the task and, with angry glances at Corbett, interfering clerks, chose another spot where they shovelled once again. Corbett turned his back on them and looked across the still frozen fields until shouts and cries behind him made him turn back to the city ditch.

"They have found the corpse, Master Clerk!" the bailiff

shouted. "Come and have a look!" Corbett moved over, noting that the face of the bailiff was almost a whitish green and even the labourers had moved away.

The bundle they had disinterred lay upon the rim of the ditch, Corbett took out his dagger and, holding his cloak firmly over his nose and mouth, began to slit the cheap, soggy canvas covering. The corpse lay as it must have been before it was bundled up and dragged through the streets on a crude sledge to be buried in the dirt and slime of the city ditch. It was naked except for a loincloth, all the clothes and jewellery had been stripped from it, probably, Corbett guessed, by the bailiff and the labourers. The stench, even after a few days, was rank and offensive and he had to stop himself gagging as he studied the corpse. The eyes were shut but the mouth sagged open, the tongue still caught between the teeth, the skin was dirty white, puffed and damp, the belly slightly swollen. He studied the purple weal around the dead man's neck and the violet bruise just under the left ear where the noose knot had been tied. There were no other marks of violence about the man except for faint purplish bruises on both the man's arms just above the elbows. He then took careful note of the man's height and, with a sigh of relief, got to his feet.

The bailiff approached. "Are you finished?" he asked.

Corbett nodded. "Yes, bury him."

The bailiff turned and shouted an order to the labourers and, within minutes, the corpse was dumped back and covered in mud. Corbett picked up a piece of wood, snapped it in two and then lashed them together with a piece of rotten rope to form a crude cross, which he stuck in the mud where Duket was buried.

The bailiff objected. "The man was a suicide!" he spluttered. "He does not deserve a hallowed burial!"

"The man was not a suicide," Corbett retorted, weary

with the day's work. "And even if he was, he was still a man." He delved into his purse and handed over some coins. "Your work is finished. You may go."

The bailiff was going to object but he looked at the clerk's tense face, remembered the powerful warrant he carried, and so kept silent, pocketed the coins and, calling over to the two labourers, turned and trudged back to the city.

Corbett watched them go and, making the crude cross secure, began to recite the Psalm for the dead. "Out of the depths, I have cried to thee, O Lord. Lord, hear my voice." Above him, a crow wheeled cawing raucously and Corbett wondered, not for the first time in his life, if the prayer could be heard and, even if it was, did it really matter?

Corbett returned to his lodgings later that day, took out his writing-tray, inkhorn, quill, pumice stone and roll of cheap parchment. This he cleaned methodically turning the rough vellum into a smooth writing surface before beginning to write down carefully the conclusions he had reached on examining Duket's body earlier in the day.

First, the corpse bore the usual marks of a hanged man. The deep red weal of the cord round his neck and secondly, the purple or violet bruise under the left ear. But what were the marks on his arms? The bruises just above the elbow? And how did they get there? Corbett put his pen down. The bruises could, he thought, have come from the fight Duket had with Crepyn in Cheapside, but it would have been the most remarkable of coincidences if Crepyn had managed to strike Duket on both forearms exactly in the same place. Moreover, the palms of Duket's hands were white and unmarked. Surely a man who was slowly choking to death would at least try in the throes of his death agonies to grasp the rope, perhaps even loosen the cord round his neck?

Finally and most importantly, Corbett thought, how could Duket have hanged himself from the chair? He had measured Duket's body and compared it to the rough measurements he had taken in Saint Mary Le Bow. A child could see the difference. Duket was too small to reach the bar. True, he could have thrown the rope over the bar but how did he secure the knot? Corbett thought back to those bruises he had seen on Duket's forearms.

No, he concluded, the only possible explanation is that Duket did not commit suicide in Saint Mary Le Bow but was hanged in such a way to make it appear as if it was suicide. Someone else tied that noose round the iron bar in the church, and had put the noose round Duket's neck, taken away the chair and pinioned Duket's arms behind his back, dragging him down to hasten his death agonies. Hence those bruises on Duket's arms. Corbett made a rapid calculation. There must have been at least two or three people involved in such a murder. But why did Duket not cry out? How did the murderers get into the church? How did they get out?

Corbett sighed and wrote his conclusions: Lawrence Duket was murdered in the church of Saint Mary Le Bow by persons unknown, for reasons unknown, and in a manner unknown. He threw the pen down and stared at the meaningless conclusion while his mind began to drift back to The Mitre and the ravishing beauty of Alice atte Bowe.

Seven

Of course, Corbett returned to The Mitre over the next few days. Ostensibly he came 'on the King's business' but his real reason was to see Mistress Alice. The burly giant and his confederates knew this and so did Mistress Alice. Corbett did not care, he felt alive in her presence, free of the Chancery, the drudgery of each passing day and the pressure of the task entrusted to him. Sometimes he sat in the tavern or the small room behind it. When the weather turned fair, they walked in the garden. Alice cultivated herbs, sage, parsley, fennel, hyssop as well as leeks, gelves and onions. There was a pear tree with a sprinkling of early spring blossom, a plot of fine grass with the surrounding soil well tilled and expecting, so Alice remarked, an abundant crop of roses, lilies and other flowers when summer did arrive.

Alice talked about her former life; her youth as an orphan, a ward of old, distant relatives. Her marriage to Thomas atte Bowe, her early widowhood and her survival in the hustle and bustle of London's wine trade with Bordeaux and Gascony. She was well versed in politics and shrewdly assessed King Edward's policies towards the Capetian Kings of France whose possible interference with Gascony and their claims of overlordship over the Duchy could plunge both countries into war and so wreck the wine trade and her profits. She alluded to the huge giant and other men whom

Corbett had seen round the tavern as 'her agents and protectors'. She gently questioned Corbett about 'the King's business' he was on but then changed the subject, as if it was rather too boring or hurtful to listen to.

Corbett spent hours at the tavern. He talked as he never had before about his training in Oxford, his work as a clerk, his military service, his wife, Mary, and his young child gone, in what seemed to be a twinkling of an eye, taken by the plague. The pain of such a loss came out as if Alice was his confessor, prising open all the secrets of his mind. Sometimes, he would just sit and play the flute, solemn tunes, love songs or dances and reels, while Alice twirled and danced. Her body slim and smooth turned and moved with the music until both were breathless either at the tempo of the music or their own laughter. Then they would eat, dishes famous for their delicacy and flavour; muscade of marrow, baked herring, pike, lamprey, porpoise roasted on coals, fresh sturgeon and dates, jellies, or light dishes, hot apples and pears with sugar, wafers with hippocras and always the best wines to drink.

The days passed into a week and then another. Corbett became tired of the tavern and so he and Alice went walking through the streets of Cheapside. On one occasion he took her to the horseshows at Smoothfield, or Smithfield as it was vulgarly called. Here, every Friday, there was a wonderful show of the best horses for sale. Horses trained for ladies, the great coursers for knights, and mares with shapely ears and necks and erect, plump haunches. Alice admired them all, particularly the young colts prancing and kicking about with their ungainly legs. The noise and smell was almost overwhelming. Soldiers, merchants, and the armed retainers of great lords moved from one group of horses to another, arguing and shouting prices with the owners.

On another occasion, arm-in-arm, they went to watch a

mummer's play in Cheapside and laughed at the antics of the clown with the great phallus and the blundering knight on his sorry nag. Then, they would move on to a cockfight or a bear-baiting show. Corbett did not like the latter with the huge animal, fierce pink eyes glaring at the dogs who would fasten themselves on him only to be shifted in a flurry of fur and blood as the bear clawed, growled and tossed himself free. Nevertheless, Alice would enjoy such sights, eyes intent, she would cry support for both bear and dogs. Corbett did not mind, he enjoyed such outings, proud of the beautiful woman alongside him and more than aware of the envious glances of other men.

Time and again, however, Alice would return to Corbett's profession, his work in the lawcourts and his special task which he now tried to forget. After all, what matter if two rogues met, one knifed the other and then later hanged himself? Such crimes were common everyday occurrences in London, and so he hid his doubts and believed the picture he had formed about the events in Saint Mary Le Bow. He was happy, content and unconcerned about Burnell or the Chancery. Indeed, he reminded himself that he had enough wealth to leave his post, a small price for the happiness he had now found. Nonetheless, Alice kept asking him and Corbett considered taking her to the courts at Westminster but thought of Burnell and changed his mind. Instead they went to the Guildhall and the city court which sat there.

He used his influence to gain access and thus hear the case of two impostors, Robert Ward and Richard Lynham. This precious pair, although well able to work and had their tongues to speak with, pretended that they were mutes who had been deprived of speech and went around the city carrying in their hands an iron hook, pincers and a piece of leather shaped like the part of a tongue, edged with silver and bearing the inscription "This is the tongue of Robert

Ward". With such instruments and different signs, they
tricked many people into believing that they were traders
attacked and plundered by robbers, who had stripped them
of their tongues as well as their goods, using the very hook
and pincers these two now carried around with them. They
claimed that all they could do was make a horrible roaring
noise. The court soon proved this was a tissue of lies for
both men could talk freely with the tongues they were born
with.

Consequently, they were sentenced to stand in the pillory
for three days with the offending hook, pincers and
counterfeit tongue slung around their necks. Alice laughed
so much that Corbett had to almost carry her out of the
Guildhall. She later confessed she found the law better sport
than all the mummers' plays. She mocked the authority of
the King and Church to such an extent that Corbett
suspected she was one of the Populares, a radical, a follower
of the dead de Montfort. Corbett was not too surprised. The
city was full of them, friends and acquaintances in the
Chancery and Exchequer were tinged with such sympathies
even though de Montfort was dead, his body hacked to
pieces and fed to the dogs some twenty years ago.

Of course, Corbett and Alice became lovers, a kiss at first,
an embrace, a meal late in the evening when the tavern was
closed. Then, almost as if they were man and wife of many
years, Alice took Corbett by the hands and led him up to her
own room. A spacious room, almost like a solar, with large
cupboards, chests, a table and stools on a polished floor
covered in woollen rugs. The walls were green, spattered
with gold stars and the small painted heads of men and
women. There were small, capped braziers and freshly cut
boughs to perfume the room with their fragrance. Alice led
Corbett over to a huge, low-slung bed and then, turning her
back demurely, began to undo her gown, slipping it over

her shoulders, removing hose and petticoats until she stood naked, a pool of lace around her. Corbett smiled when he saw that she had not removed her small black silken gloves and went to pull one off but she smilingly removed his hand and began to undress him in turn while he admired her diminutive Venus-like body.

Corbett had never experienced such passion and skill as he did that night. Time and again her lips sought his while her body enticed and drew him into a dark whirlpool of passion until eventually their bodies locked and twined together into an embrace, fell into the deep dreamless sleep of lovers. The next morning Corbett woke to find her up, dressed and fresh and lovely as any bride. She sat beside him on the bed, laughing and teasing him and disappeared when he threatened to repeat the performance of the night before. Deep in his soul, however, Corbett knew that the idyll could not last. The burly giant, Peter, stared at him murderously every time he entered the tavern while the group of men, Alice's "protectors and agents", closely watched him. They made no attempt to approach him – or he them. In fact, Alice took every precaution to keep them apart, Corbett did not care, dismissing their quiet malevolence as simple envy and jealousy.

The Chancellor, Burnell, however, kept sending Corbett sharp, brusque letters demanding reports on what progress he was making. Corbett never replied, secretly hoping that the matter would lapse and be forgotten and was rather surprised that the King's chief minister should still be interested in the suicide of a pathetic little man like Duket. It was Couville who brought him up sharp. One night, a few weeks after he had first met Alice, he returned to his lodgings in Thames Street to find a leather pouch waiting for him. The mistress of the house muttered something about it being delivered earlier in the day. Corbett took it to his room and, breaking the seal, drew out a long roll of aged vellum and a short covering letter from Couville which he tossed onto the bed. He then sat and unrolled the long scroll. It was yellow with age, frayed and cracked at the edges and the fine Norman-French writing was quite faded, though still legible. He skipped the usual flowery phrases, discerning that it was a report from one of the under-sheriffs in the city to the Chancellor of Henry II. Looking at the end of the report, Corbett saw the date above the old cracked seal, 'Written at the Tower – 2nd December in the 28th year of the King's reign' which, he quickly calculated, was 1182. He took his own writing-tray and began to transcribe the main substance of the report.

"It was early in the summer of this year that one William Fitz-Osbert, a traitor and a man of evil life, began to gather people together in a coven bound to Satan, rejecting Mary's son, as he termed Christ our Saviour. This son of the devil held coven meetings beyond the city walls and, because of the absence of our good King Henry, even within the city itself. It has been established that Fitz-Osbert and his retinue celebrated secret rites, the Black Mass, in which they committed desecration of the Host and abominably treated the sacred vessels, statues and crucifixes stolen from churches in London. Fitz-Osbert preached and proclaimed that his Master, the Anti-Christ, was coming, who would sweep away the evil, as he termed the King, Holy Mother Church, and all the pillars of government and law in the country. Time and again their secret ceremonies were performed at houses in the city or deserted ruins around the Tower where they plotted to destroy the government of the King. Secret supplies of arms were smuggled into the city to equip his followers and Fitz-Osbert stirred the people up by preaching at St. Paul's Cross, he even had the temerity to take over the churchyard gardens of St. Paul's Cathedral as if they were his own fief or holding.

"The Bishop of London bitterly complained about these practices and placed Fitz-Osbert and his followers under interdict, but that evil man simply burnt the letter and promised to do the same to the sender. Whereupon the Bishop asked the Mayor and Sheriffs of London to clear Fitz-Osbert from the churchyard of St. Paul's and place Fitz-Osbert and all his coven under arrest. Just after Michaelmas in this same year the sheriffs, constables and militia from Walbrook and the Ward of the Cordwainers attempted to clear the churchyard of St. Paul's but were beaten off with considerable losses by Fitz-Osbert and his followers. Consequently, the Mayor petitioned the Lord Chancellor to use his writ to move soldiers from Dover and Rochester Castles, as well as levy men in the surrounding counties of Middlesex, Essex and Surrey to deal with the problem.

"On the Eve of All Saints, when it was established that Fitz-Osbert and his coven would be engaged in abominable and secret practices within the churchyard of St. Paul's, the forces of the King attacked the said place. This perpetrator of all evils, however, together with his lieutenants, counsellors and close companions, many of evil repute in the city, fled from St. Paul's along Cheapside and occupied the church of Saint Mary Le Bow. The rector, Benedict Fulshim, gave them secret comfort and counsel and allowed them to take over the church. It was also later proved that this Benedict Fulshim had given permission for Fitz-Osbert and his confederates to perpetrate their secret rites in the church, supplying them with consecrated hosts as well as sacred vessels for their blasphemous practices. Once in the church of Saint Mary Le Bow, Fitz-Osbert's contingent fortified the steeple with bows, arrows, axes and swords and managed to beat off any soldiers sent against them.

Accordingly, it was decided that bundles of burning sticks should be pushed through the windows of the said church in the hope that this would drive Fitz-Osbert and his coven back into the street. Once this was done, and not without loss of life, Fitz-Osbert and all those in the church attempted to flee but all were arrested and placed in the Tower.

"Two days later, under writ from the Chancellor, they were placed before the Justices of the King's Bench at Westminster. Fitz-Osbert refused to accept their authority, cursing the name of the king, the church and that of Christ, vowing that Satan would deliver him. The Justices sentenced Fitz-Osbert and nine of his followers to be drawn by the heels to Smithfield and there hanged in chains above a fire. Fitz-Osbert and his adherents kept up their cursing and pleas to their Lord (or so they termed Satan) to come and deliver them. God's justice and the king's, however, was done. Fitz-Osbert and his confederates being burnt alive at Smithfield and their ashes scattered in the city ditch.

"This Fitz-Osbert was a man of good birth and education. He was of medium stature and of swarthy countenance; the King's Justices established that he had spent part of his life in the east where he first became acquainted with the Black Arts amongst the infidels of Syria, known as the Assassins. He claimed he was chosen specially by Lord Satan and wore Satan's mark upon the palms of his hands; namely, two inverted crosses. Purple scars upon the palms of his hands. His wife, Amisia, and their children were also members of his coven but they escaped and the most scrupulous search by the Mayor and Sheriffs revealed no trace of them."

Corbett finished transcribing and studied the report of this long dead city official before rolling it up gently and slipping it back into its leather pouch, satisfied that his earlier suspicions about Saint Mary Le Bow had been correct. He picked up Couville's note in which the old man apologized for the long delay and wished him well with his search, adding an ominous postscript that his former pupil's lack of commitment to the task assigned him was causing gossip and concern amongst his former acquaintances at the Chancery. Corbett accepted this warning, realizing that for the last few weeks he had been under Alice's spell and that he must reassert himself and complete the task, even if it was the last thing he did as a royal clerk. In all things Corbett was a professional. The long hard years of training and work in the Chancery and in the King's Bench compelled him to complete tidily and satisfactorily the matter in hand.

Eight

The next morning Corbett rose early and made his way back to Cheapside and the church of Saint Mary Le Bow. A slatternly woman, who announced that she kept house for the priest, stated that the rector was absent but, if he wanted, Corbett could wait. The clerk made his way across the churchyard and entered the main door of the church. It was deserted. Everything was as normal. The Blessed Chair was back in its proper place. No trace remained of the violent crime which had been committed there, the chairs and the benches were still stacked against the wall, so Corbett wrapped himself in his cloak and sat at the base of one of the pillars just inside the nave of the church. He crouched there staring at the long black iron bar from where Duket had hanged himself and then at the Blessed Chair back in its proper position before the high altar.

Something suddenly caught his attention. He rose, went up the church and moved the Blessed Chair to where he had found it the last time he had visited the church after it had been moved by Duket in his supposed suicide. Corbett placed the chair as closely as he remembered it from last time, then stood on it and stared at the long metal bar above him. Satisfied, he got down, moved the chair back and turned to go back down the church, almost shouting with fright at the black-gowned figure which appeared before him.

"Good morning, Master Clerk. Did I scare you?"

Corbett stared at the pale, sallow features of Bellet, the rector, trying to look calm while he endeavoured to soothe the panic which had set his heart pounding.

"No," he lied. "I was simply studying the place where Duket died."

"Ah, yes, Duket. I understand you have been very busy on this matter."

Corbett caught the sarcasm in the priest's voice and saw the smirk on his pale thin lips. He hated this man who was staring at him as if he was some sort of conspirator, as if this priest knew something unpleasant. A joke at Corbett's expense. "Yes, Master Priest," Corbett said deliberately. "I have been very busy reading a report about William Fitz-Osbert and the abominable rites he committed in this church." He felt a surge of satisfaction as he watched Fitz-Osbert's name wipe the smirk as well as any colour from the priest's face.

"Oh, have I frightened you, Master Priest?" he asked. "Surely you know about Fitz-Osbert? He can do little harm now being burnt to death over a hundred years ago." The priest's nervousness was almost tangible. A fine sheen of sweat had appeared on his forehead and he kept wiping the palms of his hands along the dirty black robe he wore. Corbett watched him closely. "What is it, Master Priest?"

The rector turned slightly, looking around as if he expected someone in the far shadows of the church to be listening. "Nothing," Bellet whispered. "There is nothing the matter. I just cannot see that Fitz-Osbert's death has anything to do with the suicide of Lawrence Duket."

Corbett patted the man gently on the shoulder. "Oh, Priest," he said softly. "Duket did not commit suicide. He was murdered and I intend to see the perpetrators suffer for their crime."

He walked round the priest and strode out of the church leaving the rector in the cold darkness behind.

Corbett intended to go straight to The Mitre but, just as he turned out into Cheapside, he felt a hand grasping his arm. He turned quickly, instinctively going for the knife in his sheath, only to find himself staring into the round bland face and cornflower-blue eyes of Hubert Seagrave, a leading Chancery clerk. Corbett had always disliked Hubert with his spiteful tongue and vicious way of hindering anyone who might oppose his preferment in the royal service. He was the last person he expected to see in Cheapside and Seagrave was clearly enjoying his astonishment and dismay.

"Master Corbett," he lisped. "How good to find you here. You have led us quite a dance. You were not at your lodgings, nor even at The Mitre." The slight sarcasm in his voice swilled through his words like dirt through clear water.

Corbett bowed in mock deference. "And you, Master Seagrave? I never thought you had legs. The only time I see you, you are either on a stool or on your knees licking the boots of some great man!"

Seagrave's fat face flushed with annoyance as he jabbed a stubby finger into Corbett's chest. "It is you, Master Corbett, who are going to need to lick a few boots! Our master, Lord Chancellor Burnell, is rather tired of sending you letters and is very angry that you have not approached him. Consequently," he continued ever so sweetly, "he has entrusted me with the task of bringing you to him."

"And if I do not come?" Corbett could have bitten his tongue as soon as the words were uttered, for he saw the quick movement of Seagrave's eyes and knew that was the answer this fat pompous fool had wanted.

"Master Corbett," Seagrave replied. "I will not take you. That is why the Chancellor sent the gentlemen who are standing behind you."

Corbett turned and saw a group of royal serjeants in the livery of the King's own household standing behind him and another standing a little far off, holding a group of tethered horses. Corbett brought his hand as hard as he could upon Seagrave's shoulder and watched the pain quickly remove his opponent's supercilious expression. "Then, Sir Messenger Boy!" Corbet exclaimed, "if the Chancellor wishes to see me, then we had best waste no time."

Corbett mounted the horse the serjeants had brought for him and then, in the middle of the group, was led along Cheapside through the shambles where the butchers' stalls and the slaughterhouses polluted the air with their rank smells. They turned left to go down Old Deans Lane, then into Bowyers Row, south along Fleet Street, passing Whitefriars, the Temple, Gray's Inn and the rich timbered houses of the lawyers, before joining the main approach to the palace and abbey of Westminster. Once they had arrived there, the serjeants, taking their mission seriously, pushed their way through the crowds, accompanying Seagrave and Corbett into the main hall, past the courts on either side and into the same small chamber where Corbett, a few weeks earlier, had received his assignment.

Burnell was waiting for him, sitting behind his desk. He continued to examine a document and allowed Corbett and his escort to stand waiting for a while before he groaned, sprang up and tossed the document onto the floor to join an ever-increasing pile of parchments there. The Chancellor then sat back in his chair, steepling his fingers together while he looked thoughtfully and rather sadly at Corbett.

"Master Clerk," he said slowly. "How good it is to see you. How kind of you to come." Then he brought one hand slamming down on the table. "How stupid and how irresponsible of you, a trained clerk, to tarry so long over the King's own business! Who, Master Corbett, do you think you are?"

The object of his anger simply stared back at him, so Burnell turned to Seagrave. "Where did you find him?"

"In Cheapside," came the smug reply. "I think he was on his way to see his mistress at the tavern."

Burnell turned back to Corbett. "Were you?" Corbett swallowed his anger and shrugged.

"Seagrave could never tell the truth, my Lord," he replied. "Even if it meant it curing the pox he undoubtedly has!"

Burnell cut short Seagrave's yelp of outraged innocence. "Thank you, Master Seagrave," the Chancellor said softly. "You have done your task well. Now you may go." The offended clerk turned and glared at Corbett and gracelessly left the room. The royal serjeants-at-arms followed him, doing their best to conceal their satisfaction at seeing such a pompous clerk deflated.

Once they were gone, Burnell gestured to a stool. "You had better sit down, Corbett," he muttered. "From what I can gather, you must be exhausted from your labours, though so far I have seen very little fruit of them." Corbett sat and braced himself for the coming storm but, instead, Burnell got up from his chair and walked across to close the chamber door. He turned and hoisted himself up to sit on the corner of his table and looked down at the clerk.

"Master Clerk," he said softly. "You may believe that the task I set you was a minor one. You may well ask yourself, and probably have, why the death of a stupid runt like Duket should concern me." He stopped and stared at a point above Corbett's head before continuing:

"It concerns me because it concerns the King. We are not talking about a stupid feud or paltry brawl but treason against the Crown, against the very person of the King!" The Chancellor fiddled with a ring on one of his stubby fingers and then stared hard at Corbett. "You do know the law of treason covers those who do nothing to prevent treason being carried out? You, Master Clerk, fall into this category and you do know what happens to traitors?"

Impervious to many threats, Corbett could only shudder at the menace in the Chancellor's words. Edward I had devised a new punishment for those guilty of treason. A defeated Prince David of Wales had been the first to experience it only a few years before. The Prince had been captured and brought to London. He had claimed he had fought against a foreign invader but the Royal Justices had ruled that Edward I was King of Wales, so David had been guilty of rebellion against his liegelord. He had been sentenced to be dragged by the heels through the mire and mud of the London streets to the scaffold at The Elms. There he had been hanged by the neck until half dead, his body then being cut down and cut open. The heart being plucked out before his head was struck off and his corpse quartered as a warning to all others who might think of plotting against the Crown.

Corbett, bravely concealing the panic and terror he felt, looked directly into the podgy face of the Chancellor. "I am no traitor," he replied. "You cannot accuse me of a crime I know nothing of." He dug into his wallet and pulled out the warrant he had been given. "Your commission says that I am to investigate the suicide of a London merchant in a London church. It says nothing of treason. Nor have I, in all my investigations, discovered anything faintly tinged with disloyalty to the King, never mind outright treason!"

The Chancellor smiled at Corbett's cold and clever reply, heaved his bulk off the table and went back to sit in his chair. "Of course, you are right, Hugh," he replied, for the first time ever using Corbett's Christian name. "You were sent into this task blind but you were chosen deliberately because of the very qualities that you have so far failed to display. A sharp mind. A tenacity of purpose. A person loyal to the King with a heart and mind which cannot be seduced. I hoped, the

King himself hoped, that you too would come to the same conclusions we have reached, the only difference being that you would find treason, the traitors responsible for it and the evidence which would hang them. We still hope that you will achieve this, though time is no longer on our side."

Corbett breathed deeply and relaxed, aware that he was still important to this ruthless man and the even more ruthless master he served. "What can I say?" he asked. "What do you want to know? More importantly, what should I know?" He suddenly felt the anger rise in him at being assigned a task, the true nature of which had been concealed from him. "You, my Lord, sent me to investigate a suicide but did not tell me I was looking for traitors. What was I supposed to do? Blunder about in the dark until I hit something? Or worse still, become entrapped myself in something I had no knowledge of? Who are these traitors? What is this treason?"

The Chancellor pursed his lips, a born lawyer, he carefully measured out his words like a thrifty moneylender counting out coins. "We do not know the traitors," he replied; "or even the treason they are plotting. All we do know is that the Populares or radical movement which supported de Montfort has revived its strength and is plotting fresh revolution in the country and in this city, and that their first task is the destruction of the King by whatever means they can employ."

The Chancellor dug deep into the pockets of his voluminous robes and pulled out a small leather pouch, the kind Chancery clerks use to keep tags or small pieces of parchment in. He undid the mouth of the pouch, shook a small piece of manuscript free and handed it to Corbett. "Read this, Master Clerk. Study it well. We received this from one of our spies whose body was later found bobbing in the Thames. It is all he sent us before he died." Corbett undid the dirty, greasy bit of parchment. Its message was short and abrupt. 'de Montfort is not dead. Fitz-Osbert is not dead. They are both in the city and will bring down our Sovereign Lord the King.' Corbett handed the message back to the Chancellor.

"Of course, everyone realizes who de Montfort was," the Chancellor's voice hardened, "but what is more worrying is that many in this city still see de Montfort as a saviour. De Montfort was an aristocrat, but he appealed to the people, not the merchants but the small traders and journeymen who mouthed phrases like 'What touches all should be discussed by all', de Montfort insisted on calling 'Parliaments', talking sessions where the community of the realm could discuss matters. Our Lord, the King, has taken over such an idea but not in the way that de Montfort intended; he wanted the cowl-makers, the cobblers, the carpenters and the masons to take over in government not just be involved in it."

"But de Montfort died, smashed to pulp like some rotten apple at Evesham!" Corbett exclaimed. "He, his family and his followers were destroyed by the King!"

"No," Burnell replied. "Many survived, spread their radical theories and still do here in London, exploiting the city's dreams and aspirations." He stopped and picked up a piece of parchment. "This was pinned to Saint Paul's Cross yesterday. Listen!" Burnell jibed, opening the crumpled greasy vellum. "Know you, Citizens of London, how you are despised and ill-treated by the endless greed of the Lords and the King. They would take from you, if they could, your share of the daylight and tax the very air you breathe. These men, the King, and his Spanish Queen to whom we render forced homage, feed on our substance, have no thought but to glitter with gold and jewels, build superb palaces and invent new taxes to oppress this city. Their priests are no better, shepherds more interested in fleecing their flocks than caring for them. But the Day of Liberation is at hand when the worms of the earth will most cruelly devour the princely lions, leopards and wolves, for the common folk will destroy all tyrants and traitors!" The Chancellor finished speaking, his face slightly purple, his chest heaving.

"The writer?" Corbett interjected.

"We do not know," the Bishop angrily replied, "but this is treason! Something is beginning to rise from the dark and murky depths of this city!"

"Is that the reference to the Day of Liberation?" Corbett interrupted.

Burnell snorted. "Day of Liberation! From what, I ask you?"

Corbett thought of what he had seen while touring the shires and walking through the midden heaps of London. The common people, in one-storey, timber-framed houses, with thatched roofs and plaster walls, taxed by sheriffs, haunted by bailiffs and royal purveyors. Their lives were pitiless, he had seen a line of peasants once at the bar of an assize court at Kenilworth, standing like roosters soaked in the rain, heads hanging, bedraggled and dirty. A fellow clerk had joked that a peasant's soul could not go to either heaven or hell, for both angel and demon would refuse to carry it because of the smell. Corbett reflected but wisely forbore to answer the Chancellor and turned to another matter.

"I know about Fitz-Osbert," Corbett said. "A devil worshipper from over a hundred years ago, but what has he to do with this?"

"Fitz-Osbert was a rebel as well as a devil worshipper!" Burnell replied. The Chancellor picked up a small carved crucifix from his desk. "There are thousands of these," he began, "in castles, homes, hovels throughout this realm. There are monasteries, nunneries and abbeys the length and breadth of the country. There are cathedrals in every city, and a church in every village. Yet Christianity is only skin deep.

There is still the old religion; we met it in Wales, the worship of dark forces and the constant harking back to ancient ways!''

Burnell nodded towards the narrow slit windows. ''Even the Abbey itself is built on an ancient place of worship. Go through the records of its church courts and you'll find superstition there: the man who placed the sacred host in his garden in the hope it would ward off marauding insects: the woman who made wax images of her husband in order to cause him pain, or the countless references to people consulting witches, wizards, warlocks and the like. Fitz-Osbert lives on in such practices, he was a rebel because the Church condemned him and the Church is protected by the State. So, attack and destroy the State and the Church is vulnerable. What worries and puzzles me,'' concluded the Bishop, ''is why the spy mentioned both de Montfort and Fitz-Osbert in the same breath? What did he know? If only he could have told us more!''

''Who was he?'' jibed Corbett. ''Some poor clerk who was sent in blind, knowing nothing of the facts or the danger?''

''No,'' Burnell smiled. ''A yeoman, a squire, Robert Savel. These rebels, whoever they may be, are bringing arms into the city. A cartload was taken by stealth from Leeds Castle in Kent, others from castles round London.''

''So, Savel was assigned to find out if these arms were brought to London?'' Corbett stated.

''Exactly,'' Burnell replied. ''Savel began his investigation in Southwark, working in a hostel called 'The Scullion' in the middle of that jakes-infested quarter. He was there ten days, he sent me nothing except that scrap of paper, then he was found with his throat cut, floating face down in the weeds off Southwark bank. I only knew of his death because I had my clerks search the coroner rolls.''

''He left nothing?'' Corbett asked.

"Nothing except the note."

"Friends or relatives?" enquired Corbett.

"None," Burnell smiled sourly. "Savel was chosen because, like you, he was alone with no family or close friends. We felt he could be trusted to hunt down traitors. He was killed, so were Crepyn and Duket. I believe that all three deaths are linked, though I do not know how. But, if the mystery of Duket's death is solved, then we may be able to proceed and discover those who resent the royal control over the city and would like to throw off royal authority, turning London into a commune independent of the sovereign, like many of the cities of northern Italy. They can do this through outright revolution or, more simply, by destroying the King. Such an act would achieve their ends for her Grace, the Queen, has still not produced a living male heir."

Corbett could only agree with Burnell. Twelve years into his reign, even longer in his marriage, the King was still without a son to succeed him. Time and again Queen Eleanor had given birth to male children but within months they were dead. Small, pathetic bundles given a hasty burial here in Westminster. The Queen was pregnant again, but would the child be a male and survive? If the King died suddenly without an heir then civil war would ensue. London could rise in revolt and dictate its own terms to anyone who wished to win its support.

"Consequently, after Savel's death," the Chancellor said abruptly breaking into Corbett's thoughts, "we assigned you to this task. We believe that Crepyn was a leading member of the Populares and a member of a secret coven pledged to the teaching of Fitz-Osbert. We also know that Duket in some tenuous way was also linked to the revolutionary elements in the city. We hope, or rather hoped, that by giving you this task we might stumble upon the truth and bring any treason plotted against the King to nothing."

Burnell jabbed his finger at Corbett. "We still believe you can do that and order you on your loyalty to the King to continue the task assigned to you. Do you accept?"

Corbett nodded. "I accept, and I apologize for the time I have lost, though I must inform you that I have made some progress. There is no doubt that Duket did not commit suicide. He was murdered."

The Chancellor's face beamed with satisfaction and he rubbed his hands together. "Good," he murmured. "Then it is surely time we caught his murderers!"

Nine

Corbett was pleased to get out of the palace, free from Burnell's strictures, warnings and secret threats. He had been investigating a suicide which was really murder which, in turn, masked treason, sorcery and rebellion. As he walked towards the river, he mentally scrutinized what he had learnt. Burnell had reached the conclusion that Duket was murdered by a secret, treasonous coven. If the reason, the method and the perpetrators were discovered then, Burnell had decided, he would also seize a nest of traitors.

He looked up at the rain-swept sky and wished he was elsewhere; on the one hand, he wanted to solve the mystery but, on the other, at what cost? A throat cut at dead of night, a violent death and a solitary funeral? Gone into the darkness without anyone really caring? He thought of Alice but, with an effort, dismissed her from his mind. Burnell had made himself clear, Corbett must act with haste to prove or disprove the Chancellor's conclusions about Duket's death. But where could he begin? He remembered Savel and 'The Scullion' tavern and decided a visit there might unveil some of the mystery.

He hired a boat at the bottom of the Westminster river steps to take him across the river to Southwark. The boatman agreed, openly smirking at Corbett who realized that the fellow thought he was just a clerk out on a pleasure jaunt, intent on drink and the soft body of some whore. He glared at the man, who simply pulled faster at the oars, a knowing grin on his face. Soon, Corbett was in Southwark, a maze of winding streets and overhanging houses. A funeral procession forced him aside, the cross bearer leading the group, chanting prayers, followed by a crier who shouted "Wake you sleepers, pray God to forgive your trespasses: the dead cannot cry; pray for their souls as the bell sounds in these streets!" The grieving mourners swept by muttering, their prayers almost drowned by the raucous howl of stray dogs.

Corbett let the procession pass and looked around. Southwark was still busy with a few hours of daylight left before those many, shadowy figures who haunted the place, came to life to pursue their secret trades and illegal businesses. In the open-fronted shops, bakers, potters, furriers and other minor traders did brisk business. The whores were there but, given the hour of the day, acted as discreetly as they could with their painted faces, braided hair and scarlet gowns. Corbett turned down one street and found himself amongst scriveners, illuminators of parchment and ink-sellers. He asked one of these for directions to 'The Scullion' but was so bemused by the complicated directions that he slipped the man some pennies and paid for a rough map to be sketched on a piece of dirty, disused vellum. Using that, Corbett arrived at a modest, two-storeyed building with an ale-stake and a crude sign above the narrow wooden entrance, proclaiming it was 'The Scullion'. He tried the door but it was locked, so he continued down the street and into a small square where a crowd surged around two large carts with boards thrown over them. It was surrounded by rough scaffolding over which were draped thick cloths adorned with religious and not so religious themes. Jesters and devils curled and twirled through enormous vines: rabbits fought knights; sacred texts trailed off into long-headed fantastical creatures; bare-bottomed monks climbed towers bearing dragons with tonsured heads; goat-faced priests chased nuns with monkey faces and slim bodies; devils and angels fought over small white souls.

Corbett leaned against a doorpost and watched the crowd mill around the makeshift stage, yelling abuse at the black-bearded Herod, laughing at the "donkey" carrying Jesus into Jerusalem as the actor inside the skin 'hee-hawed', lifted the tail and dropped huge turds on the stage. Corbett smiled and watched the devils led by a huge black Satan with a grisly mask, horns, tail and a black horse-hair suit. The creature reminded Corbett of Burnell's words about the satanic coven pledged to Fitz-Osbert and he wondered if the murderers of Duket had used black arts to get in and out of Saint Mary Le Bow Church.

He quickly cleared such a fantasy from his mind, recalling the words of one of his lecturers in philosophy: "There is nothing new under the sun, there is a cause for everything be it good or bad and these causes are, or will be, within human understanding." No, Corbett thought, Duket was killed by human cunning. If it was some secret coven, espousing the beliefs of de Montfort and Fitz-Osbert, he would find them. But what if it wasn't? If Burnell was mistaken? Or if Crepyn had been the leader and Duket's death was just an act of vengeance and now the perpetrators would simply slide back into the dark pools of intrigue which seemed to ring this city?

Corbett shook his head and looked up through the gap between the jutting gables of the houses. The sky was darkening. He did not want to be in Southwark when night fell, so he left the small square and went back to 'The Scullion'. The doors were now open, rushlights had been lit and the large, stuffy room was beginning to fill up with a strange array of customers seated around the stout wooden tables. There was a tooth-puller with pincers, bucket and pack of needles still touting for custom: a seller of squirrel skins, the dried pelts draped around his shoulders; an apothecary with skull cap and herb-bag. A forger, the 'F' brand still a resplendent scar on his left cheek.

They were joined by students and clerks from across the river, openly mocking a pedlar, a crafty-eyed, sharp-nosed man who had a tray slung around his chest which, he proudly claimed, bore the wonders of the world; one of Charlemagne's teeth, a feather from the wing of the Angel Gabriel, a phial of the Virgin Mary's milk, straw from the manger at Bethlehem, porcupine quills and the molar tooth of a giant. Corbett, grinning at the man's patter, pushed his way through the crowd towards the far end of the room where a red-haired, white-faced man in a leather jerkin and apron stood guard over the huge barrels used by the servants who rushed back and forth with dirty pots brimming with the rich brown London ale.

Corbett introduced himself and the man stared back with watery-blue eyes. "Yes, Master Clerk, what can I do for you?"

"Robert Savel?" Corbett replied. "He worked here?"

The man's eyes slipped away before he answered. "Yes, he worked here. Why? What is it to you?"

"I am, was related to him," lied Corbett. "I want to know how, even why he died?"

The man nodded to a small table in the corner. "You want my custom? Then sit down, drink, and pay for it."

Corbett shrugged, moved over and sat down, the owner later joined him with a dish of beef sprinkled with pepper, garlic, leeks and onions. A large pot of ale in his other hand. "Eat," he commanded, "and I will talk."

Corbett did as he was told; the ale was strong and tangy but the food was hot and well spiced. The landlord sat opposite and watched him. "Who Robert Savel really was," he began, "I do not actually know. He seemed well bred. I know people. I watch them and I saw through his disguise. But, he was a good stableman, he knew horses, so I gave him a job here."

"What did he do? I mean, apart from his job?" Corbett asked.

The man grimaced. "Like you, Master Clerk, he asked a lot of questions, and also went to places I would never dream of going." He leaned forward, his breath a gust of stale onions and garlic. "I am an honest man," he confided. "I liked Savel, but we all know what is going on in the city. The unrest, the plotting. I am an innkeeper, people talk and chatter in their cups, I just listen and keep my mouth shut. I want no trouble."

"So, whom did Savel meet?" Corbett queried.

"I don't know, except that he used to go out at night. Sometimes he used to talk about the Populares, the dead de Montfort and the unrest in the city. Savel tried to question people here but I put a stop to that." The man shrugged wearily. "It was only a matter of time before something happened."

"So, you know nothing about him really?" Corbett asked. The innkeeper looked around the now noisy and crowded room.

"Yes," he muttered, "one thing. He used to go and talk to an old hag who lived in a hovel down near an old, disused church by the river. This aged crone boasted that she could talk to demons and tell fortunes with her magic bones."

"Is she there now?" Corbett impatiently interrupted.

The innkeeper shook his head. "I doubt it. She was found sewn in a sack a few days ago, her magic bones thrust in her mouth and her throat slashed from ear to ear, trussed and tied she was, like a hog at Michaelmas."

"And Savel left nothing?"

"A change of tunic, that is all."

Corbett leaned across the table. "And he said nothing to you?" he asked anxiously. "Surely there was something?"

The innkeeper rubbed his mouth and concentrated on a point beyond Corbett's head. "Only a riddle," he replied. "He came back early one morning, in fact the very day he went missing. He was excited and he told me a riddle. What was it now?" The man paused, eyes screwed up in concentration.

"Oh, yes," he continued. "When is a bow which cannot be used, stronger than a bow which can?"

"And the answer?" Corbett interjected.

"Savel's answer," the innkeeper flatly replied, "was another riddle – 'when it includes all other weapons'." The innkeeper rose. "That is all. Now I must go, and so should you!" He wandered off while Corbett sat thinking about what he had learnt.

First, Savel must have stumbled on some truth, probably through the old hag who was murdered. Secondly, judging from the short note sent to Burnell, it must be connected with a secret coven of witches and rebels. But what about the riddle? Was the bow somehow connected with Saint Mary Le Bow? If it is, Corbett thought, then it's a tenuous link between a secret coven and Duket's death. His mind probed at the riddle but concluded it could mean anything. If it was a reference to Saint Mary Le Bow then it was not, at this time, worth pursuing; his task was to find the murderers and an explanation of how they so effectively carried out the assassination.

Corbett looked round the tavern, now more noisy and packed with people. The pedlar, drunk, was offering a phial containing, so he said, the Virgin Mary's tears. Corbett looked hard at some of the customers and realized it was time that he was gone. He felt uneasy as if someone evil was watching him, a malevolent presence, but it could be anyone, any of the eyes which weighed him up and then slid away when they met his. Corbett was suddenly frightened. He felt the hair on the nape of his neck curl and he fought down the urge to rise and run from the tavern. The strong ale made him sleepy and he tensed, realizing that he had to make his way back to the river bank. A woman, a whore with a blonde wig and a scarlet, loose flowing dress, came up and leaned against the table: a young girl with a sweet face and eyes a thousand years old, she lisped and promised him delights for a drink and a few coins. Corbett panicked. He rose, shoved her aside and, ignoring her stream of rich profanities, pushed through the crowd to the door. Was this, he thought, how Savel was trapped? A blow on the head, then dragged away? Corbett opened the door, entered the cold silence of the night and almost screamed as the black-haired monster approached him. Corbett stepped back against the door and watched the evil, satanic masked figure come closer.

He scrabbled for his dagger but the grotesque mask was suddenly lifted and a young, boyish face smiled at him. Corbett, weak-kneed, breathed a sigh of relief and stood aside to let the youth, Satan from the mummers' play he had seen earlier, enter the tavern.

Corbett composed himself, rearranged his cloak and withdrew his long Welsh dagger. Holding this against his chest, he began to walk through the winding rutted streets, avoiding the heaps of ordure outside each door and the open sewer which ran down the centre of the street. There were shadows deep within other ones but they saw the knife and let him pass unmolested. Corbett breathed deeply and turned into the street he knew led down to the river bank and then suddenly stopped. He was sure he had heard footsteps behind him, something quiet, slithering across the cobbles. He whirled round but there was nothing. He continued on his way, the river bank was before him.

There was torch light, a group of boatmen, the sound of voices. Corbett walked on. The sound behind him re-occurred, almost like the patter of children's feet but Corbett sensed it was something evil pursuing him through the darkness. He gathered his breath, sheathed his knife and burst into a sudden run, the night wind whipping his cheeks, his cloak flapping behind. Corbett reached the bank and almost fell into one of the barges. An astonished boatman jumped in after him, Corbett gabbled his instructions, scanning the bank for any signs of pursuit. There was none, only the silent baleful darkness of Southwark, soon hidden by a mist as the barge nosed its way across the cold, black river.

Ten

It was dark when Corbett turned into Thames Street where the fog from the river had curled inland obscuring every recognizable landmark. He was so tired and exhausted after his meeting with Burnell and the journey to Southwark, that he never even saw where the attackers came from. They were just there, muffled and hooded, stepping sideways like dancers towards him. He instinctively knew that these were not the 'roaring boys', bullies or cutthroats from the gutter but professional assassins. There were two of them, almost indistinguishable in the misty darkness, silent and dangerous, armed with long swords and short wicked daggers. Corbett unclasped his robe, rolled it around one arm and drew the long Welsh dagger from his belt. He remembered the advice of an old mercenary who had chatted about the macabre dance-like routine of professional street-fighters and, before the advice was clear of his brain, had acted upon it, sending the dagger straight into the chest of the nearest assassin.

His attacker tottered on the balls of his feet and then, with almost a sigh, slumped to his knees and pitched forward onto his face. His companion was stunned and by the time he resumed his fighting stance, Corbett had picked up the sword of the fallen assassin and was preparing to meet him. But he lacked his companion's mettle and when a casement above them opened and a raucous voice asked what was happening, he turned and fled into the mist even as the casement shut with an angry bang.

Corbett waited for a while before turning over the corpse of the fallen attacker with his foot. His knife had torn a huge gaping wound in the chest, made even worse by the man's fall. Corbett withdrew his dagger, wiped it clean on the dead man's tunic and pulled the hood from his dead assassin's face to reveal staring eyes, close-cropped hair and pox-pitted cheeks. Corbett had never seen him before, though he guessed that the man was an ex-soldier turned professional murderer. He felt nauseous at his escape, sheathed his dagger and, leaving the corpse for the scavengers, continued warily to his lodgings.

His banging awoke his sullen landlord, who looked surprised when Corbett demanded a jug of wine and a cup, and brought them without demur. Corbett grabbed them, muttered his thanks and climbed the stairs to his garret. There, he sat on his bed and poured himself a generous cupful of the wine but only drank when he was certain his trembling had ceased. He considered the danger he had just come through, recognizing that the attack was planned and wondering who had the resources to mount it. Corbett sat, chin in hand, his tired brain going round and round like a stupid dog chasing his tail. Burnell was wrong.

Corbett felt out of his depth in the murky, treacherous depths of city politics. This was not the Chancery, white-walled clean-smelling redolent of wax, ink and freshly scraped vellum with everything neatly filed and ordered. He knew that world and was at home in it. Now, he was out of his depth even with Alice. He was still deeply attracted to her but even there he felt something was wrong, threatening, though did not know what. He needed someone to rely on, someone to protect his back, someone to lead him safely through the maze of the city's underworld.

The next morning Corbett, refreshed, turned once more to the problem, but it was not until early in the afternoon that an idea had formed in his mind. He returned once more to Westminster and sought an urgent audience with Burnell. The Chancellor was preparing to travel to meet the King at his palace of Woodstock outside Oxford. The carriage and carts were being organized and marshalled in the palace courtyard and, though on the point of departure, the Chancellor stayed to hear Corbett's request and, despite his puzzlement, immediately granted it. A clerk was called, the required letter was written out, hot wax poured on it, the Chancellor even had his own seal brought back to validate the document and so silence any questions it may provoke. Corbett then bowed, muttered his thanks, and, after requisitioning a horse from the palace stables, rode north along Fleet Street to Newgate Prison.

The prison was really a collection of buildings, small towers along the old city walls bounded by the odiferous city ditch. Their overall command was under the nominal custody of a keeper and other officials often no better and sometimes much worse than the prisoners within. In theory, the city granted money and alms towards the upkeep of the prisoners but in actual practice, very little of this money reached the inmates. Not that any of them were there long enough to experience the people's generosity. Justice was swift and the phrase 'tried on Wednesday, hanged on Thursday' was correct. The prison was divided into debtors, aliens and felons. The latter experienced the worst conditions, cramped, two or three to a cell, or the many pits beneath ground. Every week these pits were emptied, the prisoners drawn up, shackled and put into carts to be taken to The Elms or Smithfield to be hanged.

The prison officials were engaged in just such an exercise

when Corbett arrived. The carts were already half full, the greasy, black-garbed gaolers impatient to be off. The prisoners, young and old, stood like stunned oxen, listless, dirty, frightened, yet eager to get on, to be through with the nightmare and so be done with it. Corbett immediately used his warrant from Burnell to halt the proceedings while he walked amongst them, a living man amongst the dead. He looked at their faces, the evil, the bland, the good, the innocent and, above all, the young. He felt a terrible compassion for them all and used his influence to get the young taken back to the cells, abruptly informing the keepers that the Chancellor himself would review their cases. Then he continued his scrutiny until he found the person he was looking for, a youth of about sixteen or seventeen summers, black tousled hair, with a filthy face and clothes, though there was a mark of defiance and sardonic amusement in the clear blue eyes.

"What is your name?" Corbett asked.

"Ranulf. And what is yours?" came the quick reply. The voice was sharp with a city accent.

"I am Hugh Corbett, Clerk in the Court of the King's Bench and I may have a pardon for you!" The blue eyes shifted and the boy turned and spat.

Corbett shrugged. "So, let it be. Hang if you wish!"

"Wait!" Corbett turned back. "I am sorry," the boy's face was suddenly young and frightened. "But what do you want?"

"I need your help," Corbett replied. "I need you to lead me through the sewers of this city, and I am not talking about those that run beneath our feet." Corbett looked around; "But those we stand in."

Ranulf grinned. "Then I am your man."

"Good!" Corbett turned to the gaoler who was hovering nervously behind him. "There," Corbett said, handing him the document that Burnell had drawn up. "Fill in the blank space. This is a pardon for all crimes past and present of Ranulf ... " Corbett stared questioningly at the boy.

"Just Ranulf," the youth replied.

"Ranulf atte Newgate" – Corbett concluded. The keeper nodded and barked a few commands which soon had the boy released from his chains and the rope removed from his neck.

Corbett immediately seized the boy by the shoulder, put his arm around him and almost ran him out of the prison yard. He hurried his new-found assistant into the street, then turned into a dark alleyway strewn with offal and reeking of stale blood from the nearby slaughterhouses. Here, Corbett put Ranulf up against the urine-stained wall and, drawing his dagger, held it so close to the boy's throat that a small jewel-pinprick of blood appeared on his skin. Corbett watched the surly arrogance be replaced by fear, then spoke softly and slowly:

"Master Ranulf, I have just saved you from hanging for what?"

"Theft, housebreaking," the boy croaked. "It was the third time."

"Then," Corbett said, "it will be the last. Stay with me. Help me and you will be a free man. Betray me and I will see you die very slowly. Do you understand?"

The boy nodded, his eyes mesmerized by the long steel blade of the dagger so close to the neck he too thought he had just saved. Corbett smiled, released his grip and walked back into the main street, his faithful shadow sidling behind him.

Corbett spent the rest of the morning and the early afternoon ensuring that Ranulf was clean and tidy to sit with. He took him into the same tavern where he had earlier stabled his horse, made him strip off his dirty rags, wash

himself down in a tub of water purchased from a bemused
landlord and then left him there wrapped in a blanket,
hungrily eating while he went out and bought him clothes, a
plain tunic with a green capuchon, hose, boots, a belt, purse
and a small evil-looking dagger in a leather sheath.

When he returned, he found Ranulf gone, only to find
him in one of the outhouses of the tavern, completely naked
enjoying the plump body of one of the tavern maids whose
squeals of delight led to Corbett's discovery. The clerk was
tempted to abruptly end his minion's fornication but
sighed, realized the youth was celebrating his new-found
freedom and returned to wait in the tavern. A short while
later Ranulf, wrapped in his cloak, sheepishly entered to
receive a sharp lecture from Corbett which he promptly
forgot in the pleasure of trying on the new clothes Corbett
hurled at him.

Once Ranulf was dressed, they both left the tavern and
made their way down Cheapside. It was late in the day, the
crowds were beginning to dwindle and a cold evening wind
was blowing away the first weak signs of spring. Peasants in
their brown smocks and wooden clogs were leaving for the
countryside, merchants with their sumpter ponies and
empty carts trying to get out of the city before the curfew was
imposed, the pedlars and journeymen busily concluding
their business for the day. Corbett led Ranulf into The
Mitre, urging the boy to keep close as he peered through the
fading light for Alice.

"She's gone. Mistress Alice is not here today." The giant,
Peter, suddenly blocked the way, his small red-rimmed eyes
glittering with malice.

"Will she be back this evening?" Corbett asked anxiously,
wondering where Alice could be, his disappointment at not
meeting her mingled with concern for her safety. The man
pursed his lips and shook his head.

"She's gone. She'll be back tomorrow. But she's gone now, as you must be, Clerk, or I will call the watch. The curfew begins soon."

Corbett, swearing softly to himself, turned and left. He found Ranulf outside, a short distance from the tavern. "Why did you leave so quickly?" Corbett asked sharply. Ranulf hunched his shoulders.

"You may not recognize him, Master Clerk, but that Peter is an executioner. He used to top people, hang them. He was an executioner at The Elms." He looked strangely at Corbett. "Your mistress," he continued, "keeps strange company."

Corbett agreed, Ranulf's words making him all the more anxious about Alice's safety. He turned and made his way along Cheapside, turning the problem over in his mind with Ranulf almost running behind, quietly cursing as he tried to keep up with his new protector's long-legged stride.

Of course, at Thames Street, Corbett had difficulties with the lady of the house, who looked suspiciously at Ranulf and rather strangely at Corbett trying to persuade her that his new companion was his assistant. Ranulf did not help matters by grinning evilly at the woman but eventually Corbett and her reached an agreement; Ranulf would be given an even smaller garret at the back of the house but until it was cleared, he would have to sleep on the floor in Corbett's room. Ranulf seemed happy enough with the arrangement though, when they reached Corbett's room, he produced a bunch of keys that he had furtively stolen from the lady's belt.

Corbett went down to return them with a rather lame excuse and then came back to give his crestfallen assistant a stern lecture which ranged from honesty to the horror of The Elms. Then he told Ranulf what business he was involved in, watching the boy closely for any reaction. But, apart from remembering Peter at The Mitre as a former hangman, Ranulf knew nothing of Duket's murder. He recognized Crepyn's name and said he had a reputation of being a powerful man with one foot in the respectable world of the Guildhall and the other in the dirty gutter of London's underworld.

Corbett also questioned the youth on his earlier life, being surprised at his speech which betrayed a thin veneer of education. Ranulf's explanation was short and brief. His parents had been respectable people from Southwark who had died in one of the many epidemics which ravaged the city. He had been left as an orphan in the care of an elderly aunt who was also the mistress of the local priest. The latter had given him some schooling before Ranulf threw off any attempt to control him, running wild with gangs of young men before slipping into crime and the many opportunities it presented in the city. The rest, Ranulf concluded, Corbett knew.

The clerk looked at the freshly scrubbed face of the youth who should, if justice had had its way, now be hanging by his neck at The Elms, black-faced, tongue protruding, body broken. Corbett smiled. He was glad he had saved Ranulf and threw him a cloak, telling him to sleep for tomorrow, he promised, would be a busy day.

Eleven

The next morning Corbett nudged Ranulf awake and sent him down to collect water and breakfast. Corbett dressed and opened the shutters of his window and, though there was a faint sparkling silver on the roofs and eaves of the surrounding houses, the sun had broken through the early morning frost. It would be a bright day. Corbett wanted to leave the matter in hand and go down to visit Alice but then he remembered Burnell, cursed quietly and, opening his trunk, lifted out his writing-tray with a sheaf of freshly scrubbed vellum and placed them gently on the lid of the trunk. Ranulf returned, grinning wickedly, and Corbett guessed that he had clashed yet again with the mistress of the house; her sullen arrogant manner seemed to bring out the worst in the youth.

Corbett washed and made Ranulf do the same before they broke their fast on the weak ale and rye bread the boy had brought up. As they ate Corbett outlined what he wanted Ranulf to do, gather supplies, collect the horse Corbett had stabled in Cheapside, return it to Westminster and then carry out a secret task which made the young man's face go white with fear.

"What are you trying to do?" he screeched. "Send me back to Newgate and a hempen collar!"

Corbett reassured him that all would be well while he

would protect him from any consequence. "Though," he added wryly, "you are too professional to be caught."

The boy looked balefully at Corbett, muttered some obscenity and was still murmuring when Corbett opened the door and pushed him downstairs into the street.

Corbett then sat on the bed with the writing-tray on his knee and he thought for a while before starting on his report.

"The death of Lawrence Duket. Date of death 13th or 14th January 1284. Place: Saint Mary Le Bow, Cheapside. Lawrence Duket was a goldsmith who lived off the Walbrook. His business was moderately prosperous. A respected citizen, a member of the Guilds of Goldsmiths. He was not married, had no family except a sister. There is nothing to link him with any secret organization in the city. To all appearances, he was certainly no member or supporter of the Populares party. His relationship with Ralph Crepyn is tenuous. The latter was a man who rose from obscurity to the rank of Alderman in the city. He was a notorious moneylender and gained most of his wealth in the money market. He had sympathies for the dead traitor, Simon de Montfort. He had links with the secret Populares party and even more shadowy ties with the criminal fraternity in the city. It would appear that about midday on the 13th January Crepyn met Duket in Cheapside, sharp words were exchanged, blows struck. Duket, surprisingly for such a placid man, suddenly drew his dagger and, either by luck or mischance, struck Crepyn a mortal blow, driving his dagger deep into the moneylender's throat. He then withdrew the dagger and, before the hue and cry could be raised, fled along Cheapside into the churchyard of Saint Mary Le Bow and managed to grasp the handle of the church and so claim sanctuary. The Rector of the aforesaid church, Roger Bellet, granted him this, leading him up into the sanctuary and the safekeeping of the Blessed Chair. The priest, according to law, provided him with a candle, flint, a jug of wine and a penny loaf of bread. The said priest also according to custom, had the church locked by himself on the outside

and bolted within by Duket himself.

There was no hue and cry or posse sent to the church as the city law officers had not time to arrange this because of the proximity of Saint Mary Le Bow to the scene of the homicide. However, the city Ward did set a guard outside the door of the church not so much to ensure anyone broke in but to ensure that Duket did not attempt to flee by night. The said guard later reported that no one approached the door, nor did they hear any disturbance in the churchyard during the night. They kept their watch until Prime when the Rector came to the church and unlocked it. However, he could not open the church nor rouse Duket by shouting or pounding on the door. Accordingly, he and the Watch used a log lying nearby to force the door open. Inside, the scene was as follows. There was no mark of violence or disturbance in the entrance, or nave of the church. In the sanctuary, however, the Blessed Chair had been moved far to the right beneath the large window. There are two of these windows, either side of the sanctuary, each has an iron bar projecting out beside it with a curled hook on the end to hang garlands or sanctuary lamps. On that particular morning, the one on the right bore the dangling corpse of Lawrence Duket.

It would appear that Duket had gone down to the entrance of the church, taken some disused rope from the bell tower, gone back to the sanctuary and, moving the chair over, hanged himself from the metal bar. The Coroner was called with the Jury of the Ward to examine the corpse. They questioned the guard placed on the church and accepted their statement that no one entered or left the church during the night, nor did they see or hear anything suspicious. The Coroner put them on oath that they fulfilled their duties faithfully and conscientiously. I now believe they spoke the truth. The Coroner and Jury also examined the Rector of the church who claims he knows nothing of Duket's death. The Coroner accepted this but I have great doubts about the man. Nothing I can prove but a feeling of deep disquiet. Duket had died by strangulation, there was a deep purple ring about his neck caused by the rope and a bruise beneath his left *ear caused by the knot in the noose. His body bore no other marks except bruises on the forearm and a shred of linen caught between his teeth. The Coroner noted all this as did I when I exhumed the body from the city ditch.*

The Coroner and Jury also investigated the cause of the quarrel between Duket and Crepyn in Cheapside. They believe it was caused over Jean Duket, Lawrence's sister, whom, it was alleged, had been seduced by Crepyn. I have questioned the aforesaid Jean and I believe the quarrel did not concern her. The Coroner concluded that Duket had been guilty of the unlawful homicide of Ralph Crepyn and had fled for sanctuary to Saint Mary Le Bow where he had committed suicide.

Do I accept such a verdict? If Duket had survived he could have done two things. First, sued in the King's court either by himself or through an attorney that his attack on Crepyn had been in self-defence. If such a plea had been accepted, Duket would have received a pardon. Secondly, if Duket had not pleaded in the courts, or had and had his plea rejected, he would have had to abjure the realm. This would have meant walking on the King's highway, carrying a small cross, to the nearest port. In this case, the Steelyard or some other dock along the Thames to secure passage abroad. In view of Duket's wealth, this would not have been too difficult and the same wealth would have ensured a comfortable exile until he secured his safe return. So why did he commit suicide?

First, to escape the hangman's noose? However, he was in sanctuary and had other more palatable choices open to him as I have described above. Secondly, to avoid being adjudged a felon for the death of Ralph Crepyn and so risk all his property being judged forfeit to the King? But first he would have to be convicted as such and, secondly, he had no kin except a sister with whom he was scarcely close. Thirdly, that his mind became sick and he could not cope with the guilt of what he had done? Or, he was overcome with dread and fear of Crepyn's associates who would surely exact revenge? This might prove the more acceptable solution if I could find that Crepyn did have close associates for he seems to have been a lonely man, bereft of family, friends or close colleagues.

Nevertheless, I do believe that Lawrence Duket was murdered on the night of 13th January 1284 by person or persons unknown. First, I cannot accept that a man who fled for safety in the sanctuary of a church, (who therefore wanted to protect his life) would later decide to end it in such a macabre way. Secondly, and more importantly, Duket could not have stood upon the chair and tied the noose around the projecting iron bar. I have measured the man's corpse and have found he was too short. He could simply not reach the bar above him to tie the knot. To conclude, I believe Duket was murdered but many questions remain unanswered.

Item: For what reason?

Item: By whom?

Item: How did they manage to enter the church and leave it without using the door? The priest could have let them in but they would still have needed Duket's co-operation from within. They would also have had to either suborn the watch, distract or overcome them, and there is not a shred of evidence to indicate this.

Item: The murderers could have been given entrance to the church by someone else but that person would have had to have a key to the outside lock or stolen the Rector's yet there is no evidence for this.

Item: The only way any person could have entered the church was by the side door but this was firmly locked and has been for years, there was no sign or evidence of it being opened. Another way would have been through the windows, but most of these are too small. The large ones were firmly clasped and could only have been opened from the inside. None of these windows showed signs of being forced. There is no indication or sign of any secret entrance to the church.

Item: If person or persons unknown had secured entrance to the church their movements would have aroused the attention of the watch. Surely Duket would have resisted and screamed for help and not gone to his death as quietly as a lamb to the slaughter?

Item: What were the black silk threads still tangled in the noose, *the piece of linen caught between Duket's teeth, and who inflicted the bruises on Duket's forearms?*

Corbett finished his report and re-read it, studying his conclusions carefully. The clear picture he had constructed a few weeks ago was there – Duket was murdered though Corbett glumly realized that he had made little or no progress on how, by whom and for what reason. He was still poring over the manuscript when a crashing on the wooden stairs outside startled him. The door was flung open as Ranulf burst in.

"No wonder," Corbett sarcastically commented, "you were so unsuccessful as a housebreaker. You're as gentle as a charging war horse!"

Ranulf, red-faced, breathlessly apologized and, putting the supplies he had bought on the end of Corbett's bed, slumped down against the far wall to rest himself.

Corbett watched him for a while. "Were you successful?" he eventually asked.

Ranulf nodded. "Oh, yes, I broke in to both Duket's and Crepyn's houses. They were both deserted, both stripped to the bone if not by the executors, then the professional thieves who always mark down such buildings for investigation! Duket's had nothing, absolutely nothing and I only found this in Crepyn's house."

Ranulf brought from his wallet a tattered, yellow piece of parchment and handed it to Corbett, who studied it carefully. The drawing was quite clear, a simple, crudely devised pentangle under an arch with a date, as one would find on the end of a letter, "30 April 1283". Almost a year ago. Corbett threw the piece of parchment behind him. "Is that all?"

"That is all!" Ranulf glared at him. "I risked my neck going into both houses. For what? A dirty piece of parchment which you immediately toss away!"

Corbett smiled. "No, I am grateful. Look," he handed
the youth a few coins. "I want you to get something to eat
and, at the same time, find out something for me." He
raised his hand to quell the expected objection from Ranulf.
"It is not as dangerous as the last but more important. You
say you know the underworld?" He saw the look of
perplexity in Ranulf's face, "The criminals of this city," he
explained.

Ranulf nodded, warily watching this strange clerk.
"Good," Corbet continued: "Then I would like you to find
out two things. First, a few evenings ago two murderers,
professional assassins tried to kill me a few yards from this
house. They were not 'roaring boys' or gutter bullies but, as
I have said, skilled assassins specially hired. I would like you
to find out who hired them and why? Secondly, my young
friend, if I was attracted," he glared at Ranulf, "and I am
definitely not, but if I was attracted to young men and boys,
where would I go to in this city?"

Corbett watched with quiet amusement the scared look
on Ranulf's face. "Do not worry," Corbett said softly. "I am
not that way inclined and, even if I was, you would have no
cause to worry!"

"I am not worried," Ranulf was almost shouting. "I'm
frightened. What will happen to me if I'm caught in such a
place? If the church does not burn me, my friends might and
I do not want to become the laughing-stock in every
alleyway in the city!" He glared fiercely at Corbett, who
smiled sweetly back.

"Ranulf, I have every confidence in you." He looked
towards the door. "Now you had better go!"

The young man pulled a face, rose and clumped towards
the door.

"Oh, Ranulf," Corbett asked. "What did you do when
you broke into a house? Go barefoot?"

The reformed housebreaker grinned. "You are dull in some things," he replied. "We wore mufflers. Rags tied round our boots. Everyone knows that!"

"Except me," Corbet smiled. "Well, you had better go!" Ranulf went carefully down the stairs, cursing and muttering but secretly wondering at the strange habits of Master Corbett. Behind him he could hear the faint notes of the flute, soft and sad, telling of dreams gone, lost or shattered.

Twelve

Ranulf did not return that day nor the next morning when Corbett, washed, barbered and dressed in his best robes left to see Alice at The Mitre. Corbett thought and dreaded that she might not be there, but she was, fresh as a May morning in a dark blue dress, with a copper chain slung low round her narrow waist and a simple gold necklace round her throat. Her hair was as soft as silk and he smelt the perfume as she flung her arms round his neck, her body soft and sinuous against him. He was relieved to see that the burly threatening Peter was not about and would have taken her directly upstairs but she protested most demurely, saying that she was busy, it was not the right time. So he accepted her excuses and sat in the kitchen while she served him wine and sweetmeats, chattering all the time, fending off his eager hands and parrying his questions. Instead, she asked how his investigations were going and laughed when he grimaced, digging his face deep into the winecup. "I hear you have a bodyguard?" she pouted. "Should I be jealous?"

Corbett stared at her and then laughed. "No, he is just a boy," he replied. "A messenger, a carrier of goods." Alice smiled and passed on to other matters. Corbett watched, aching for want of her as she busied herself about the kitchen in everyday chores. He sensed, for all her happiness, a tension as if her gaiety was forced. He was also puzzled, troubled by something she had said or left unsaid, but could not decide what it was. At length, he decided to leave; Alice was evidently too busy and he began to feel that he was impeding her. So he rose, embraced her passionately and left the tavern for the sunlit street of Cheapside.

Restless and ill-at-ease, he pushed his way through the crowds down past Cheapside and into Poultry to the house of his banker, the goldsmith. The front of the shop was down and the stall pulled out to display a fine range of products. Apprentices busied themselves about, taking privileged customers within to view more precious objects while others kept an eye on the not so privileged. The goldsmith was inside but came out when Corbett sent a message in with one of the apprentices. He looked troubled and evasive. "You want me, Master Corbett?"

"Yes, and some information, Master Goldsmith."

Guisars looked round to see if anyone had heard Corbett before beckoning him into the shop. "What is it?" he whispered. "What do you want?"

Corbett stared into the frightened man's eyes. "Duket? Crepyn?" The man's eyes fell away.

"Crepyn," he answered slowly, "was a well-known member of the Populares party. He kept the coffers of the party and often asked us for money. Protection money to safeguard our houses. Some paid, many did not. Duket may well have refused."

"But it was Crepyn who was murdered," Corbett pointed out and the merchant looked at him.

"Was it, Master Clerk?" he replied hoarsely. "Crepyn deserved what he got but Duket? Suicide?" he shook his head. "Never!" he said emphatically.

"Is there more?" Corbett asked softly. The goldsmith again shook his head and pleaded with his eyes for the clerk to go.

It was late by the time Corbett reached his lodgings to find that Ranulf had returned, exhausted, dirty and fast asleep on the floor wrapped in his cloak. Corbett let him sleep a little longer while he lay on his bed and thought about Alice's lovely, naked body, her long, black hair flowing round her like a veil. If only he could search out and lay to rest the anxiety in his heart. Corbett heard Ranulf stir, so he swung his legs off the bed and shook him awake.

Ranulf yawned and woke, scratching his head as he peered at Corbett through puffy, sleep-laden eyes. "Master Clerk," he yawned, stretched himself and shook himself fully awake. "Master Corbett," he urged. "You must be careful. You must not go out by yourself as you did today!"

Corbett looked at him. "Tell me why, Ranulf! Tell me now!"

"Have you ever heard of the Pentangle?" Ranulf asked.

"No, nothing, except the drawing you brought to me a day ago from Crepyn's house. Why?"

"I know very little myself," Ranulf replied, "except that it's a secret society here in London involved in the Black, er Black ... "

"Arts? Magic?" Corbett testily interrupted.

"Yes, that's right. There's many here in London. Usually a few fools but this is different. Very secretive. Very powerful. They are led by someone called 'The Hooded One'!" Ranulf stared pityingly at Corbett.

"Anyway, they are the ones who have marked you down. Those assassins who almost did for you the other evening. They were hired by this group. You were very lucky. It's because you not only escaped but killed one of them that has provoked a lot of interest in what you call the criminal frat..., criminal... "

"Fraternity!" Corbett impatiently interrupted.

"Yes, fr ... fraternity. Anyway, they may well try again."

Ranulf looked quizzically at his master expecting to see fear, even terror and secretly marvelled at the man's composure. Ranulf had no illusions about what he would do in Corbett's place, a swift journey to the docks to buy an even swifter passage abroad.

Corbett's equanimity, however, was only superficial. He was frightened, more than he had ever been in the thick of the fighting in Wales. Killers were stalking him here in London and they could strike at any time. He looked up at Ranulf. "And the other business?" he asked.

"Much better," Ranulf replied. "There are a number of places, usually outside the city limits. I found a few but one in particular where Duket himself went. He evidently liked young boys and his favourite works there. Should we go tonight?" Corbett shook his head.

"No, go back to sleep," he ordered wearily. He then extinguished the candle and rolled himself up in his robe like a fearful child, brooding on the nightmares around him.

The next morning, exhausted after a restless night's sleep, Corbett gave Ranulf a message to be taken to Burnell and made the youth repeat it till he had learnt it by rote, before going down the stairs and into the street. Ranulf went first and Corbett was about to follow when Ranulf suddenly pushed him, sending him sprawling back into the passageway, the door slamming in front of him. Corbett heard a series of dull thuds on the door, drew his dagger and waited for it to open. He heard Ranulf shouting, the door opened and Ranulf re-entered.

"In the name of the Good God, what is the matter?" Corbett yelled at him.

Ranulf shrugged, opened the door and pointed to the ugly squat crossbow bolts deeply embedded there. "I saw them up on the roof of a house where it sloped down to

meet the next building," Ranulf replied. "I don't know why
I looked. I heard a noise and stared up. They had the sun at
their backs, I could hardly see but I saw their crossbows so I
pushed you back and dropped to the ground." He looked
down at his mud-spattered tunic. "I cannot understand
your wish to be clean!"

Corbett smiled at the young man's pathetic attempt to
amuse him. He suddenly felt wearied, tired of this task, weak
with relief at the death he had so narrowly escaped. He sat
slumped on the stairs, head in his hands as Ranulf watched
him anxiously, not knowing what to do. Corbett felt the
same. He knew that he would have to move out of Thames
Street if he wished to survive. They, the Pentangle, or
whatever other nonsensical name they called themselves,
wanted him dead! They knew where he was and twice had
attacked him here. Corbett thought of asking Alice for
shelter but that was too close, it might put her under risk.
Burnell had placed him in this danger, then Burnell could
assist him. He looked up at the still waiting Ranulf.

"Go upstairs," he said softly. "You will find a set of
saddlebags behind the chest. Put the contents of my chest
into them and whatever else you may think we need. I will
settle accounts with our hostess."

While Ranulf clattered back upstairs, Corbett went to see
the owner of the house, explaining that he would be away
for a while but handed over money to keep his lodgings. He
did not inform her where he and Ranulf were going but told
her to keep any messages sent to the house. She looked
anxiously at him but his face forbade any questions so she
shrugged and accepted his words. Corbett then left, taking
wry amusement from the thought of how the lady would
react when she found two crossbow bolts embedded in her
front door. He went nervously into the street but it was
deserted as were the surrounding rooftops which would

have provided his assassins with the perfect escape route. Ranulf was waiting there with bulging saddlebags. Corbett made him repeat the message he had given him earlier, then added a brief few words which Ranulf, eyes closed and face tight with concentration, faithfully repeated to Corbett's satisfaction.

At the end of Thames Street they parted, Ranulf for the river and Westminster, Corbett north to Cheapside and Saint Mary Le Bow. Despite his tiredness, Corbett decided to walk and the fresh morning air revived him. He felt better, stronger in himself and angry at the secret killers who stalked him through the streets. Corbett now made sure he was in or near a group for he knew that he was most vulnerable when he was isolated in some lonely place. He had decided to go to Saint Mary Le Bow for it was here where the trouble had begun. Those who had tried to kill him, wanted to stop his investigations into Duket's death. So, if he was to prevent his own murder, he would have to solve the mysteries of that man's death. Moreover, Corbett sensed he would be safe in or near the church. His attackers had murdered Duket but they would certainly baulk at committing a similar crime in the same place. Such an act would bring the whole power of the Crown and Church crashing down about them.

The thought comforted Corbett as he pushed open the gate to the overgrown churchyard and made his way to the main entrance. It was locked, so Corbett strode over to the priest's house and hammered on the door. The Rector answered and the astonishment on his narrow face told Corbett that this man expected him dead and he felt the anger and fury rise like bile in his throat. "Priest!" he had to restrain himself from shouting. "I need the keys to the church!" The priest, flustered and concerned, said he would open the door but Corbett thrust out his hand, snapping his

fingers as a sign that the keys should be handed over.
Nervously, Bellet removed them from the cord which hung
from his belt, Corbett grabbed them and, turning on his
heel, strode over to the church.

Once inside, Corbett began to look for secret entrances,
doors or passage-ways. House of God or not, he spared
nothing in his search. He tried the disused side door and
realized it had been blocked up for years. He checked the
walls, windows and jabbed with his dagger between the
sandstone pavement slabs. He could find nothing, so, he
moved into the sanctuary, ignoring the protests of the priest
who had joined him, and poked beneath and behind the
altar. He went down into the crypt, dark, smelly and cold, to
examine the floor, walls and thick granite pillars, but there
was nothing.

Corbett, hot and tired, then went outside walking around
the perimeter of the church looking for signs of forced
entry. There were none, no break in briar, bramble and
rank weeds, except beneath one small window, Corbett
found strands of cloth hanging from a thorn bush which he
picked and rubbed between his fingers. They could have
come from anywhere and, as he had surmised in his report,
the window above could have only been entered by a young
boy and, only then, with Duket's permission. Corbett put
the fragments of cloth into his purse and walked back to the
main door of the church where the Rector was still waiting.

Bellet had regained his composure and was standing with
a smug, slightly sardonic expression on his face. He did not
say "I told you so" but his whole stance and bearing seemed
to proclaim it. The clerk was about to leave when he
remembered something he had seen as he walked past the
church's cemetery. "Your burial ground?" he asked. "It has
many fresh graves, judging from the newly turned mounds
of earth?"

The priest shrugged. "A bad winter brings many deaths," he replied. "Why, do you wish to investigate them as well?" Corbett ignored the jibe, gave a slight bow, and turned away out of the church into Cheapside.

He found Ranulf at the appointed meeting-place in a tavern on the corner of Walbrook and Candlewick Street. The reformed housebreaker was busily gawking at every woman in the place when Corbett joined him and the clerk had a difficult time making him concentrate on handing over the information he had. Surprisingly, Burnell had seen Ranulf immediately, and told him to return late that afternoon with his master. "Did he say anything else?" Ranulf shook his head and buried his face into a tankard.

"No," he replied, "except to say that when you come, he would have something for you. Oh, he did say that we should leave Thames Street and go to the Tower." Corbett groaned inwardly, though he realized that the Chancellor was right. He could no longer stay in the city where he was so vulnerable. Sometimes he felt that he was being followed, being watched, but whenever he looked around, he saw no one and dismissed his suspicions as the fantasies of a fevered brain.

Corbett wearily urged Ranulf to his feet, ensured he was still carrying the saddlebags, left the tavern and, passing by the church of St. Stephen, went down Walbrook. This was where the skinners plied their trade with their tubs, shears, knives and threads. Animal skins were pegged to wooden frames outside every shop or beside every stall while the skinners, knives in hand, scraped away the dry fat from the inside of the skins before throwing the finished piece into a tub of water to soak. In other places, the skins were being tanned, or fully finished, being sewn together into rectangular shapes of standard size.

Corbett watched all this, trying to divert his mind and

calm his frayed nerves. He wished he could scrape away the lies and fashion the truth from the many deceits he had discovered. Was there a finished product he wondered, or would he stay floundering in a morass of doubt until the assassins reached him or, until Burnell dismissed him ignominiously from his task? If only he could find out why Duket stabbed Crepyn. If only he could discover how the murderers, for there must have been more than one, had gained access to the church and then so easily escaped. There was one other problem. Why was Bellet so confident? Why did it always appear that the priest knew he was coming, even more, almost sensed that Corbett was stumbling around in the dark? Like some jester in a mummer's play, put there for the quiet laughter of the onlookers?

Thirteen

Corbett was still trying to solve the problem, almost talking aloud, arguing with himself when, their long walk was over, and Ranulf and he found themselves on Bridge Street walking down to the river with the fortified gate and mass of London Bridge rising ahead of them. They did not approach the bridge but turned off down an alleyway which led to the river where they secured passage on a boat to Westminster. Corbett was not looking forward to the coming interview with the Chancellor and wished he could go back to The Mitre, the soft, calming embrace of Alice's body and be done with this matter once and for all.

Yet, like a man in a dream, he left the boat when it docked and followed the well-worn path to the Great Hall, envying the clerks writing quietly in their stalls or scurrying about on some important business. He reached Burnell's room and, taking a deep breath, asked the clerk outside to announce him. The man went ahead but returned followed by the pompous Hubert, who dismissed Ranulf with almost a girlish flicker of his eyes and thrust a leather chancery pouch into his hands. "The Lord Chancellor has had to leave," he loudly proclaimed. "He has gone to join the King at Oxford. He asked me to leave you this and," he extended a sealed writ, "these orders."

Hubert glared at Corbett. "Well," he snapped. "Aren't

you going to open the letters?"

Corbett smiled, realizing that Hubert did not know what was in the document and was probably dying with curiosity to find out. "No," Corbett replied slowly. "The Lord Chancellor gave me specific instructions not to open these in the presence of any junior clerk!" He then turned away and walked down the Great Hall, Ranulf trotting behind, with Hubert rooted to the spot, looking as if he was suffering from an attack of apoplexy. As he walked, Corbett opened the writ and found that it was simply a licence to reside in the Tower and have the right to leave and enter whenever he wished.

Ranulf, walking behind, quietly groaned at the weight of the saddlebags, tired of the aimless walking about and wondering where he would spend the night. He wished, despite the crossbow bolts, that he could go back to Thames Street. He thought of the lady of the house and almost groaned with pleasure. She was sulky and arrogant but he had seen the way she had looked at him and knew he could possess her. She might be a grand merchant's wife with her swaying hips and gartered hose but, on a feather bed with those legs about him, he would make her happy. Yet, not now and he almost cried when he followed his inscrutable master into the boat and instructed the oarsman to take them to the Tower Wharf.

Despite his mood, Ranulf decided to enjoy the journey, exchanging ribald insults with the boatman while Corbett sat and stared moodily into the water. The boat passed the Baynards Castle, the Steelyard and other craft, long and small, still making their way along the river. Eventually, the boat sped under London's house-laden bridge with its nineteen arches each protected by starlings, wooden boat-like structures which prevented boats crushing into the hard stone arches. Then on, past Botolph's Wharf,

Billingsgate and the Wool Quarry until they berthed under
the soaring stone mass of the Tower.

The formidable rings of walls, fortresses and towers
dominated the south-east corner of the capital and
overawed both Ranulf and Corbett as they crossed the moat
and went through successive towers, many of them in the
process of being redeveloped, into the inner ward which
surrounded the four-square, central donjon or White
Tower. Corbett and Ranulf were challenged as they
approached each gateway but, on producing Burnell's writ,
Corbett and his companion were allowed to proceed. In the
inner ward, a burly Yorkshireman, a serjeant from the
garrison, told them to stay, while he went looking for the
Constable, Sir Edward Swynnerton. He was gone a while,
leaving both men in the freezing cold to stare about them
and take in their surroundings.

The bailey round the White Tower was quiet though
Corbett could see that the building operations in the Tower
would begin again in the spring. Bricks were stacked round
the huge kilns where they were made, sand and gravel were
strewn across the ground and huge oaken beams lay in
lop-sided heaps. The Tower was almost a small town in
itself. Rows of wooden stables, a pigeon loft, open-fronted
kitchens, barns and hen coops all huddled together round
the walls. There was a small, bare tree orchard in one far
corner and the wood and plaster houses of the officers of the
Tower in another near the main entrance. Corbett moved
across to where Ranulf was staring at a derelict Magonel,
when a tall, silver-haired austere man, wrapped in a thick
brown military cloak approached and introduced himself as
Sir Edward Swynnerton, Constable of the Tower. Corbett
introduced himself and Ranulf, showed the Chancellor's
writ and briefly explained why they had come to the Tower.
The Constable stared hard at Corbett and looked as if he

was going to protest but then he scratched his grizzled head and summoned a guard to take Corbett and Ranulf to a sparse chamber in the White Tower.

Once there, Ranulf, exhausted with all the walking, curled up on his straw-stuffed mattress and fell asleep while Corbett lit the two candles in the room to read the report that Burnell had left for him in the leather chancery pouch. It was written in the Chancellor's own hand.

"Robert Burnell, Bishop of Bath and Wells and Chancellor of England, to our trusty and well-beloved clerk, Hugh Corbett, greetings. I have read your letter and noted its contents. I believe this reply and the information it contains will be of use to you.

Item: the drawing of the Pentangle found in Ralph Crepyn's house (and we will not ask how you came by it!) is not unknown to me. The Pentangle is a sign used in magic and the black arts. It is often drawn by the Magician or Witch on the floor or table as a symbol of protection when summoning Satan or some other diabolic power. Of course, it is one thing to summon the rulers of the demonic kingdom and another if they actually come. Nevertheless, those who practise the black arts and dabble in magic pose a threat to Holy Mother Church and in doing so pose an even more dangerous threat to the safety and security of the throne. There is no doubt that members of the Pentangle also include adherents of the radicals who still support the ideas of the dead de Montfort.

"Item: Simon de Montfort's father was a Crusader and fought for the Cross in Palestine and other lands in Outremer. De Montfort also led Crusades against the Albigensians in Southern France, whose heretical practices were supposed to be secret, closely linked to necromancy and sorcery. I merely tell you of this to draw a link between rebellion and those who exercise black magic with their secret name, 'The Pentangle'!. Although the de Montforts were resolute Crusaders, there is no doubt that they may have become infected by the very diseases they tried to destroy.

"One such disease was the cult of the Assassins. These belonged to

a secret Muslim sect whose headquarters lie in the impregnable fortress of Alamut in the valley of Kazvim in Persia. They are controlled by their chieftain, The Mysterious and Sinister Man of the Mountains, who commands a network of strongholds throughout Persia, and even in the Holy Land itself. He commands a core of devoted terrorists who murder by treacherous violence. It would appear that the de Montfort family came into contact with this cult and may have adopted some of its practices. Assassination of an anointed king by the followers of black magic is, as you know, not new in England. It is alleged that William Rufus died at their hands in the New Forest; Richard I may also have been a similar victim, and other more fruitless attempts were made upon the person of the late Henry III, the present King's father.

"The de Montforts undoubtedly used such methods. After Simon de Montfort was killed, almost thirty years ago, his son, Guy, escaped abroad. It is perhaps no coincidence that while our present king was on a Crusade in Palestine an assassin attempted to kill him in his own tent with a poisoned dagger. Our king was only saved by the speedy and faithful ministrations of his wife and doctors. On his way to Palestine the king's cousin, Henry of Germany, visited Viterbo in Sicily and went to Mass at the Cathedral Church there on the 13th March 1271. Guy, Simon de Montfort's son, ignoring the sanctity of the occasion and the place, stabbed Henry to death before the high altar.

"Item: The date, 30th April 1283, is significant only in that it is one of the great feasts of the Satanists and probably the day the Pentangle met. The scrap of paper probably being a writ which convened the meeting, though it is ample proof that Crepyn was a member of the coven. The important factor is who sent it? Who is there in the city who embodies and represents the traditions of de Montfort and Fitz-Osbert?

"Item: To draw all this tangled skein together it is certain that the adherents of de Montfort and Fitz-Osbert are still active in the city fomenting rebellion and plotting the assassination of the King and

*members of his council. They expose their masters' ideals and are
prepared to further them through practices like murder and black
magic. They are the Pentangle and I urge you not to dismiss them
lightly as harmless fools for they pose a great threat and their treason
is even worse than that of their dead masters".*

Corbett studied the manuscript, threw it to the floor and
wrapped his cloak tightly round his body. He had no reason
to dismiss Burnell's warning. Those very assassins that the
Chancellor had mentioned were now pursuing him, fully
intent on his death. He looked round at the thick granite
walls of the tower room and, despite the cold and squalor,
felt safe and secure enough to fall into a dreamless sleep.

Fourteen

A few hours later a servant roused Corbett and Ranulf with food and drink, a mess of stewed meat and vegetables and two stoups of rather watery ale. Ranulf grumbled but ate the meal avidly as if it were his last, answering Corbett's questions on where they were going with a mouth full of food which put Corbett quite off his own meal. Once Ranulf had finished, Corbett sent for Swynnerton and asked for horses and a military escort into the city, not because they feared attack but so as not to be arrested by the Watch for breaking the curfew. The only ones allowed to travel by night were persons going about their lawful business who had to carry a lighted torch to show their presence and Corbett did not wish to proclaim their mission for all to see.

When all was ready, Corbett and Ranulf, hooded and cloaked and preceded by a soldier, made their way out of a postern gate in the Tower and, keeping the old city wall on their left, made their way north to Aldgate Street. The journey was uneventful though cold, and when they arrived outside the tavern specified by Ranulf, the tower guard was only too grateful to turn his horse back and leave them outside The Blackbird, a large spacious inn which, to all intents and purposes, seemed closed for the night.

Corbett and Ranulf waited in the shadows opposite the tavern until the soldier leading their horses had left the street, then Ranulf took Corbett down an alleyway which ran alongside the tavern and knocked gently on a side door, an action he repeated four times in some form of pre-arranged signal. The bolts inside were quietly drawn, the door opened slightly and a hastily whispered conversation took place, Ranulf handed over the two gold pieces that Corbett had given him and the door swung open to let them enter.

It was pitch dark inside. Corbett could just about make out the shape of the porter, he was wondering where to go next when he heard a creak and a ray of dim light seemed to spring out of the floor as a trapdoor was gently raised. Ranulf and Corbett were quietly urged to descend the ladder. Ranulf went first, Corbett coming after, astonished at what he saw and heard. The tavern evidently had a spacious underground cellar safe from prying eyes and, being directly under the tavern, was effectively sealed off from the rest of the world. The place was well lit by torches in iron sconces fixed to the wall as well as the pure wax candles on the tables arranged around the room. At first glance it seemed a normal tavern scene except that there were no windows, the air coming from narrow grilles in the ceiling and a hollowed out tunnel at the far end of the room which probably served as an escape route if the authorities ever did manage to intervene. The walls had been whitewashed, then covered in frescoes, and these gave the first indication that this was more than just a tavern.

The paintings were of young naked men or boys involved in some sport such as javelin throwing, wrestling, running or lying on couches with myrtle wreaths on their heads and cups brimming with purple wine in their hands. Despite the poor light, Corbett marvelled at the crude realism of the paintings and looked round expectantly at the people who used this place. There were not many and all, like he and

Ranulf, were hooded and cloaked to disguise themselves. They sat in pairs quietly conversing or talking softly to the young boys who served wine and ale from the large barrels stacked at the far end of the room. These boys or youths had been chosen for their good looks and, in their tight, multicoloured hose and short quilted jackets, they would please their customer as they moved, hips swaying, between the tables, their long hair curled and pressed like a girl's.

Corbett felt the sleeve of his cloak being pulled by Ranulf and realized he was standing gawking while other guests were coming down the ladder and pushing their way by him. He followed Ranulf to a small alcove and ordered wine from a boy who simpered and cast coy glances at Ranulf before mincing away. Corbett sat astonished at what he saw. He had heard of these secret taverns and drinking places but had never been in one. On the surface, it was just a secret tavern but he knew that he was in a male brothel and that all the customers ran terrible risks if they were caught, public humiliation followed by a lingering slow and painful death, which explained the furtiveness of the customers and the hidden secret ways of their meeting places.

Ranulf seemed more at ease and relaxed, accustomed as he was to living outside the law, pitting his wits daily against the normal order of society. When the wine was brought, Ranulf caught the servant by the sleeve and whispered a name. The youth glowered and pouted, picked up the few coins Corbett put down and sauntered away. A short while later another boy came over and sat down on a stool opposite the two men. His hair was the colour of corn, the face heart-shaped like a girl's with long eyelashes, pale cheeks and small, red lips. Despite his air of forced gaiety, Corbett saw the fear in the youth's kohl-ringed eyes and felt pity for this ravaged face of sixteen or seventeen summers with eyes which looked a thousand years old.

"I am Simon," the boy lisped. "I am told you wish to speak to me."

Corbett leaned over. "No," he replied softly, "but Lawrence Duket did!"

The terror in the boy's eyes was something almost tangible and he would have jumped to his feet if Corbett had not held his arm tight and whispered reassuringly that he was Duket's friend and meant him no harm.

"What happened to Duket?" Corbett whispered. "Why did he die? He was murdered wasn't he? Tell me please. I can protect you as well as bring his murderers to justice."

Simon stared at Corbett, biting his lower lip and blinking back the tears. He started to speak then bowed his head and nodded. Corbett waited until the boy raised his tear-stained face. "They murdered him," he whispered.

"Who?" rasped Corbett.

"The Dark Ones, hooded and masked, led by a giant and a dwarf," Simon answered softly. "They floated up the church. There was no sound. They simply picked him up, moved the chair and hung him up." The youth wiped the tears from his face with the sleeve of his jerkin and looked quickly round.

"I do not know where they came from or where they went," he continued hurriedly. "They must have come from Hell. Not a sound, not a word." He looked wide-eyed at Corbett. "And Lawrence did not even utter a word! Why?" he asked tearfully.

"How do you know this?" Corbett asked, trying to calm his own pounding excitement.

"I was there," the boy replied. "I fled to the church early in the afternoon. I got in through a small window as the priest was at the door."

"What about the Watch?" Corbett asked.

"They had not arrived," Simon continued. "I went over

to Lawrence and comforted him but he told me to hide. I lay down behind a bench in the sanctuary and fell asleep and did not wake till it was dark. There was a candle burning. I was going to get up when They suddenly appeared. So I hid. I was terrified and kept hidden till morning when the priest and Watch forced open the door. In the confusion I fled."

Corbett thought of the piece of fabric caught on the briar bush and nodded. "You must know more," he insisted. "Giant? Dwarf? Who were these people?"

The boy shook his head. "I must go," he whispered hoarsely.

"Tomorrow," Corbett urged. "Meet me tomorrow, just before Prime, outside the church of St. Katherine's by the Tower." The boy nodded, got up, smiled falsely and minced away.

Corbett and Ranulf sat for a while longer then, pulling their hoods closer, got up and left, their shadowy guide letting them out into the street. Corbett was pleased to be out under the stars and gulped in the fresh air to purge and clean the evil humours of that cellar. Then, satisfied that they were alone and not being followed, they turned and made their way back to the Tower. Ranulf had scarcely followed the conversation between Corbett and the boy in the cellar and so pestered Corbett with a series of questions, but then gave up when all he received were grunts and evasive answers.

Corbett was excited by what the boy had said though he realized he had only embellished what he suspected already. Duket had been murdered by more than one person. But the rest? Who were they? The Giant? The Dwarf? Figures in black who glided up the church without a sound? How did they get in? Corbett was still trying to find solutions when they reached the postern gate of the Tower and a sleepy, grumbling guard let them in. They made their way to their

new quarters, Corbett told Ranulf to shut up and stop
nagging him and, rolling himself in his cloak, turned to the
grey granite wall and willed himself to sleep, to forget the
exhaustion and terrors of the day by thinking of the soft,
satin silk body of Alice.

Corbett went along to the meeting-place the following
day after telling Ranulf to stay and rest from the previous
day's labours. He made his way out of the Tower postern
gate and walked the short distance to the church of St.
Katherine. As he approached, the bells of the church were
tolling for Prime.

He expected to find the place deserted and was surprised
to see a small crowd gathered outside the porch of the
church. He broke into a run, dreading what he might see
when he arrived. The crowd parted to let him through and
he almost fell over the body of the young man whom he had
spoken to the previous evening. Dressed in the same clothes,
his long blond hair still curled and pressed, the only
difference was the long red gash in his throat and the blood
which saturated the front of his tunic. Simon was lying there
sprawled on the ground, arms and legs stretched out, his
sightless eyes staring up into the sky.

"What happened?" Corbett asked one of the bystanders,
a small, brown, wrinkled woman with straggly grey hair
escaping from underneath her hood.

"I don't know," she replied. "A group of us were making
our way into the city to the market. We found the body here.
There was no one about. Someone has sent a message to the
Coroner and the death crier." She peered closely at Corbett,
as old women are wont to do. "Why do you ask? Do you
know him?"

Corbett shook his head. "No, I thought I did but I was
mistaken." He turned and slowly walked away, realizing that
when he had visited the Blackbird Tavern the previous

evening he must have been followed. Somebody must have seen him talking to the boy and decided to follow him.

Corbett suddenly felt tired and angry. Here he was, a king's clerk going about the King's lawful business, yet he had been blocked at every turn, attacked twice and now, whoever it was, had taken the life of this pathetic young man. He felt a deep sense of depression, he was fumbling about in the dark like a traveller who has lost his way, and was now up to his waist in a morass. Somebody knew something. Somebody would have to pay for that long red angry gash in that young man's throat. But who? Was it Ranulf? Could he be trusted? Had he been suborned or bribed by Duket's murderers? Corbett abruptly dismissed the idea as fantastic and unworthy of Ranulf's help over the last few days. After all, he reasoned, it was Ranulf who had brought him to meet the young man so it was highly unlikely that he would allow the meeting to take place and then arrange the boy's murder. The only person Corbett suspected was guilty of some crime or complicity in a crime was Roger Bellet, the Rector of Saint Mary Le Bow. The sinister priest who always hinted that he knew more than he was telling. Corbett felt a surge of anger and frustration through him when he thought of Bellet's sardonic smile and sarcastic comments. Corbett decided that he had been baited long enough. Burnell had given him complete power in this matter. It was time he used it, to his own advantage.

Fifteen

On his return to the Tower, Corbett demanded an audience with its constable, Sir Edward Swynnerton. The old soldier met him in his quarters on the first floor of the White Tower. He listened carefully to Corbett's request and sorrowfully shook his head. "I cannot do that, Master Clerk," he replied. "I cannot simply arrest a priest and detain him, even question him, without giving a reason or a warrant from the King! Can you imagine the Church's reaction to that? A rector of a London parish church taken from his house and put into the Tower! I could be excommunicated, lose the favour of the King and be removed from office. No," he concluded. "I cannot do it."

"But this man may be a traitor," Corbett argued fiercely. "He may be responsible for murder, for plotting treason against the King. For being involved in black magic. Surely no court, church or secular would agree with that?"

"That may well be so," Swynnerton replied. "But you say 'may'. You have no proof. You have no warrant and that is the difference!"

Corbett restrained his temper. He realized that his anger would only alienate this old soldier unaccustomed already to taking orders from a clerk. "What happens," he said slowly, "if I am right? If this priest is a criminal in both the eyes of the Church and of the Crown? Let us say he is involved in villainy and this latter comes to light. How can we," and he emphasized this word to include both himself and the constable. "How can we then justify not taking precautions now?" He saw doubt creep into the old man's eyes and was satisfied knowing that his cause was not utterly lost. He watched as the old soldier turned and crossed to one of the arrow-slit windows overlooking the inner ward and let him think for a while before he returned to the attack.

"You must realize, Sir Edward, that I would not make this request unless I had good cause. I suspect that this man is an accomplice to murder, involved in treason which may threaten the very life of the King. You simply cannot stand aside, wash your hands of the matter and say that it is nothing to do with you. Moreover," he added cautiously, "if I am proved correct, the King will have good reason to be grateful to you."

Swynnerton turned away from the window, the doubt and uncertainty clear in his face and eyes. He carefully stroked his small goatee beard while searching for a way out of the problem presented to him. He sighed, went to the door and summoned in one of his attendants, ordering him to call the captain of the guard immediately. A short while later, a burly, red-haired, thick-set man came into the room. He had the rugged, sun-tanned features of a professional fighting man. His very presence, dressed in half armour, and the stance he adopted when he entered the room indicated a man who would take orders and follow them to the letter. Swynnerton went over and clapped him on the shoulder.

"John Neville, may I introduce our guest. Master Hugh Corbett, Clerk in the Court of King's Bench."

Corbett felt Neville's eyes look him up and down, quietly assessing him. "Have you ever fought, Master Clerk?" The voice was clear and authoritative.

"Yes," Corbett replied. "I saw some service in the Welsh counties when the King was chasing numerous Welsh princes up and down their valleys. It was an experience I shall never forget, and to be quite candid, I am not too eager to repeat."

Neville grinned, showing a row of yellow, broken teeth. "I thought as much," he replied. "I pride myself on being able to distinguish between those who have fought and those who have not. I simply think it rather strange to have a man I judge as a fighter in the garb of a clerk."

"Master Corbett," Swynnerton interjected, "is not here to do any fighting but to ask us to do it for him. Whatever he says, do!" Swynnerton then left the room and Corbett realized that the cunning old soldier had carefully covered both bets. If Bellet was arrested and later protested, Swynnerton could claim that he had no real part in it. If Bellet was arrested and Corbett was proved correct, then Swynnerton could bask in the reflected glory. Corbett, smiling at the adroit way the constable had dealt with him, took Neville by the arm and quietly confided what he wanted him to do.

After he had finished, Corbett would have liked to have left the Tower and gone to see Alice but, as he admitted to Ranulf when he returned to their quarters, he was too frightened to go out into the streets of London. It might well have been he, not the young boy, Simon, who could be lying outside the church of St. Katherine with his throat cut from ear to ear. Ranulf received the news of the young man's death with the same nonchalance Corbett had seen that day he had chosen him from the line of condemned men at Newgate. Death was a natural order of things, a daily risk, an occupational hazard, though he agreed that Corbett should stay in the Tower. Corbett also realized that he could not leave until Neville returned with the priest and put him to the question. He shuddered when he thought of this. Bellet would be taken to the dungeons beneath the White Tower and left to the tender mercies of the torturers and their skilled finesse in extracting information from the most recalcitrant prisoners.

Corbett then spent hours waiting by a window until Neville and a company of archers brought the priest, tied and bound, into the inner ward. He did not go down to meet them but, even from where he stood, he could see that the priest, for all his anger and protests, was a very frightened man. Bellet and his escort disappeared from view as they turned down a long row of stone steps leading to the dungeons. Corbett knew he would have to wait. He wrote a short note to Alice and sent Ranulf out with it, instructing him to inform Alice that he was safe but not to tell her of his whereabouts. He knew that if she had that information, she too would be in danger. After which, Corbett wrapped his cloak around him and lay on the bed awaiting for Neville to send for him.

It had been dark for some time when Corbett was aroused from an uneasy sleep by Neville roughly shaking his shoulder. "Come, Master Clerk," he whispered hoarsely. "You had better join us." Corbett got up, relieved himself in the *garde-robe* in the corner of the room, washed his hands and face in a bowl of cold water and, drying his hands and face with his cloak, followed Neville out down to the dungeons. The soldier led him down the long row of narrow steps that he had seen the priest descend a few hours earlier. Then Neville turned right, following the line of the Tower to a small door at the base of one of the turrets. They entered and Corbet felt he had arrived in what must be the very antechamber of Hell. It was a low-roofed room, cold and damp. The torches fixed in rusting sconces on the walls flickered and spluttered and he could smell the damp earth beneath his feet mingling with the smell of smoke, charcoal, blood, sweat and fear.

The room was empty of all furniture except for open braziers clustered together at the far end, besides which were two or three small stools. There were chains and manacles hanging from the wall but his eyes were drawn to the small macabre group at the far end.

As Corbett approached, he realized that there were three men stripped to the waist, black scraps of cloth wrapped around their foreheads to keep the sweat from running into their eyes. Their bodies glistened with sweat and they kept turning to the braziers, pulling out long rods of iron, the handles wrapped in cloth to protect their hands. He saw one of them take a glowing iron bar and place it against what he thought was a shadow near the far wall until he heard a terrible scream and saw the shadow jerk and writhe. He then became aware that it was the priest hanging by his wrists from the chains, stripped of all his clothing except for a loincloth. His body was covered in long gaping wounds where the hot metal bars had been pressed. Corbett hid his revulsion, knowing that this was not the time for pity. This man may well have been responsible for Duket's death, for the death of the young boy, Simon, and for the two criminal assaults on himself. The only fear Corbett experienced was a secret dread that the man might actually be innocent.

"Has he answered the question I asked you to put to him?" Corbett rasped. Neville shook his head.

"No," he replied. "He says he had nothing to do with Duket's death." Corbett almost felt his heart skip a beat and his mouth went dry with fright.

"Has he said anything?"

Neville grinned. "He has said enough. He keeps calling on the Lord Satan to help him and that is not the sort of prayer you would expect a priest to say!"

Corbett went round the braziers, pushing his way past the torturers, who looked expectantly at him as if waiting for fresh orders to apply their burning metal bars.

He could see that their victim had had enough. Bellet's face was bloodless and the eyes crazed with pain, the thin, bony, pathetic body of the priest had reached the limit of his endurance.

"Well, Master Priest?" Corbett whispered. "We meet again, though in quite unexpected surroundings!" He went closer, almost whispering through the priest's sweat-soaked hair so only he could hear. "Lawrence Duket, did you murder him?"

Bellet turned his face slowly towards him, his eyes narrowing as he tried to swim out of the circle of pain which had engulfed him. "This is your doing, Clerk! You whoreson get!" he cursed. "You are no more than a country bumpkin. You don't know with whom you are dealing. You and your sort will soon be swept away." Bellet grunted and tried to lift his body to alleviate the racking pain in his chest and legs.

"I can stop this," Corbett said. "I can stop it as soon as you tell the truth. What is the Pentangle? Who ordered Duket's death? Who killed the boy Simon? Who ordered the attacks on me?" The priest's eyes, however, slid away and Corbett sensed he was still secretly laughing at him. Flushed with rage, he grabbed the priest by his chin, wrenching his face round so he could look into his eyes.

"Tell me," he urged. "Tell me now!" The only response he got was a stream of abuse and spittle. Then the priest's body twitched, went rigid like a man going into a fit and suddenly relaxed, the head slumping forward on his chest.

Neville came closer, pushing Corbett aside as he felt the chest and neck of the priest. "The man is dead," he said. "It is now finished." He looked at Corbett. "What shall we do with the body?" he asked.

Corbett shrugged. "Wrap it up in a shroud," the clerk replied, "and bury it among the paupers." He then left the dungeon and the gruesome figures standing there in the flickering obscure light of the braziers. He felt no remorse at what had happened to Bellet. He knew the man was guilty. He was evil and had played no small part in the murder of Duket and, by his own confession, was deeply involved in treasonable sinister activities against the King.

*   *   *

Across the black misty river the hooded figures of the Pentangle met once more and crowded round their leader, the Hooded One. They sat quiet but were gripped by an air of expectancy, almost fear. "So, a member of this group is destroyed?" one asked. The speaker to the right of the Hooded Leader's chair, nodded in agreement. "We understand that he has been taken," he replied. "He is probably dead and we have Corbett to thank for that! Our spy in the Chancery also reports that Corbett knows a great deal about us."

"Then why not kill him?" another asked, an edge of fear to his voice. "Why not kill him?" he repeated insistently. "When he meets his doxy in The Mitre, I have often seen him there … " his voice trailed off as a deathly, cold silence fell upon the group.

"We cannot kill him there and you know you should not have said that!" the speaker replied slowly. "You know the pact. None of us ever say what we are, male or female, what we do, or even what part of the city we frequent. However," the speaker's eyes glittered behind his mask as he scanned the group. "We will execute Corbett, and take vengeance for our dead comrade, but the important thing is that we continue with our Grand Design. Each of us must prepare our groups, collect arms and wait for the sign to rise in rebellion!''

"And Corbett?" came the insistent interruption.

"We have someone special assigned for him," the speaker firmly replied. "You may consider Corbett already dead!"

Sixteen

The next day Corbett went to Saint Mary Le Bow leaving orders for Ranulf to join him there. The church and house were deserted. Neville had given him Bellet's keys but Corbett, surprisingly, found the door unlocked and carefully pushed it open. The main room looked as it had the night Corbett had visited the priest so many weeks ago. The charcoal brazier was full of dead spent ash; a cup half full of wine and slivers of stale cheese, rat-gnawed, lay upon the top of the room's only chest. He knocked them off and opened the heavy wooden lid. There was a smell of must mingled with stale sweat as Corbett began to pull out clothes; a dirty robe, hose, a pair of leather boots. There was nothing else. Corbett looked around the deserted room. There must be more. He suddenly realized that there was something missing.

This was a priest's house and yet there was no cross or crucifix. He scanned the wattle-daubed walls, the crumb-strewn table, but looked in vain for signs of any religious worship. He kicked the dirty rushes with his boot and then went into the small room at the back which served as both a kitchen and buttery. It was filthy and contained a dirt-stained table, a low stool, a shelf of cracked cups and soiled wooden plates. "The man must have lived like an animal," thought Corbett. He went back into the main

room and stared at the loft at the far end which must have
served as a bedroom. There was a screen of polished wood
which protected the bedchamber from prying eyes and it
could only be approached by a dangerous-looking wooden
ladder slung against the wall.

Corbett propped the ladder up against the rim of wood
which ran along the base of the partition and carefully
climbed up. He expected to see the same dirt and chaos he
had met below but the reality was much different. The
bed-chamber was small, with a little window made of horn
high in the wall, letting in sufficient light. The floor was
polished with beeswax and thick velvet drapes hung from
the whitewashed walls which depicted the most lascivious
love scenes. A huge bed, covered in a sea-green silken cover,
occupied most of the room. Corbett climbed over the
wooden partition and sat on the bed, feeling the rich,
feather-filled mattress and bolsters beneath him. On the
near side of the bed was a wooden stool with a pure wax
candle in a silver-plated holder, while on the other, a small,
richly carved, wooden chest. Corbett leaned across the bed
to open the lid.

Perhaps it was a sound, a slight shadow, but he suddenly
rolled to the right and avoided the evil edge of the sword as
it came crashing down where he had been lying. Corbett saw
a tall dark figure dressed completely in black. A pair of
glittering eyes stared at him through the holes of the black
hood as the secret assassin lifted the sword for a second
blow. He did not wait but flung himself under his attacker's
upraised sword arm and both went crashing against the
wooden partition. At such close quarters the assassin could
not use his sword but brought its pommel brutally down on
Corbett's unprotected back. The pain was excruciating and
all he could do was keep tight hold of his assailant's waist
and force him back against the partition. Corbett hoped

Ranulf had arrived and would hear the noise, when suddenly the partition cracked and he and his attacker tumbled off the edge and went crashing to the floor below.

Corbett was lucky for his fall was cushioned by the body of his assailant who was not so fortunate. A large pool of blood seeped out from beneath the black mask and Corbett, after massaging his arms and wrists and stretching his back to relieve the soreness there, leant over and lifted the mask from his attacker's face just as Ranulf came belatedly crashing through the door, shouting at the top of his voice.

"You're too late!" Corbett snapped. "Why did you not hear the noise earlier?"

Ranulf scratched his chin. "I wandered over to the church and only heard the sound of a scuffle as I came back." He pointed down to the assassin lying on his back, one arm and leg curiously twisted. "Who is he?" Ranulf asked.

Corbett forced the man's hood off and looked down at the smooth young face, white, eyes stony beneath a fringe of black hair. A trickle of blood seeped out of the corner of the dead man's mouth and ran down to join the pool of blood caused by the skull caving in.

"I don't know," Corbett replied softly. "But he was waiting for me. They sent him. They knew that I was coming here." He stared at the anxious face of Ranulf.

"Who are they?" Corbett asked. "For God's sake what do they want from me?" He got up and dusted himself down, trying to ignore the pain in his back and arms. "Come on," he pointed to the fallen ladder. "Hold this, Ranulf, while I finish my search."

Ranulf held the ladder secure whilst Corbett went back up into the dead priest's sleeping quarters to search the carved wooden chest. It was packed with clothes, hose, jackets, robes and shirts of the highest quality, taffeta, velvet and silk, pure woollen wraps, lush fleeces, jewel-encrusted belts, soft leather boots and velvet gloves. The priest had evidently lived a double life of public poverty and private wealth. There were no documents or scraps of parchment, the only book being a leather bound copy of a bible with a gold clasp. The pages were beautifully written and adorned with small intricate drawings, a feast of colours, Corbett could appreciate the skill of the calligrapher who had carefully written the words and then brought them to life with scarlet, gold, green and other colours. He turned the pages over, there was nothing amiss except that he was surprised that even a man such as Bellet should have a bible, let alone such a costly one. Corbett carefully leafed through the pages but there was nothing there. He turned to the back of the book where the man who put the manuscript together would leave blank pages for its future owner to write reflections or meditations.

Bellet had certainly written but not spiritual aphorisms or moral axioms. There were pages of closely written Norman French or dog Latin which refuted the existence of Christ, alongside spells and incantations, as well as drawings of a man with a goat's head sitting on an altar dripping with blood under which there was an inverted cross. Another drawing showed a church full of people with the empty vacuous faces of sheep, all turned attentively towards a figure in priest's garb but with the fierce head and slavering jaws of a wolf.

The last drawing, which Corbett judged as most recent, was completely different. It showed a tower, square-shaped and on its turreted top was an archer, bow in hand, the arrow was in the air, directed along a road or pathway, on which there was a man seated on a horse with a crown on his head. The drawing was crude, almost child-like, yet it had a vigour and realism of its own. Underneath were the words *Hac Die libertas nostra de arcibus veniat.* Corbett translated it aloud. "On that day our freedom comes from the bows". He studied the drawing and the words. He remembered the riddle of the dead squire, Savel, about a bow which cannot be bent being more dangerous than one that could for it included all weapons.

The image of the freshly turned graves in the nearby cemetery became clear in his mind and, almost shouting out loud, he turned and scrambled down the ladder, the bible still in his hand which he thrust into the hands of the astonished Ranulf.

"Quick," he urged. "Take this to the Chancellor! Tell him to study the drawings at the back, particularly the last one. Tell him to stop the King coming in from Woodstock and order a search in all the fresh graves here at Saint Mary Le Bow!" Corbett made Ranulf repeat the message until he had it perfect by rote and dismissed him.

Corbett calmed himself and, after looking around the house, left, making his way across the muddy yard to the church. The main door was unlocked and he cautiously opened it and went in. He stood just inside, breathing deeply, while listening with all his being for strange or threatening sounds, trying to feel the atmosphere and determine if there was danger. Satisfied that there was none, but still shaken by the attack he had just survived, Corbett walked up the nave of the church and sat in the Blessed Chair. He looked down into the shadows of the entrance, realizing that this must have been about the same time of day that Duket had fled to the church. Once again he probed at the question of how the assassins had got into the church, murdered Duket and then escaped without notice.

He sat, continuing to look down the nave, when suddenly the solution to the problem just seemed to present itself. It was so simple, so obvious he just started to laugh, the echoes pealing around the deserted church. Of course, it was so apparent, so clear, its very simplicity showed the cunning and brilliance behind it. He remembered the voice of his old 'Dominus', Father Benedict, telling him that there was a solution to every problem. "It's just a matter of perspective, my dear boy," he used to boom out. "Just a matter of perspective." Well he had the right perspective, now it was a matter of finding who the real murderers were. The shadowy figures behind the Pentangle.

Corbett got up, walked down the church and went outside into the early spring sunlight. He felt pleased and, almost without noticing, found himself making his way to see Alice. The tavern was deserted so he quietly walked across the main room and pulled open the door to the kitchen. Alice, her back to him, was talking to Peter the Giant, his great bulk towering above her as she softly explained something to him. Corbett called her name and she spun round. The blood drained from her shocked face but then she gave an exclamation of joy and ran towards him, flinging her arms around his neck, hugging and kissing him. She grabbed his heavy brooch-clasped cloak and unfastened it while she told him to sit and sent Peter for food and drink.

"You are pleased to see me?" Corbett asked dryly.

Alice kissed him again full on the lips. "Of course!" she pouted. "Where have you been? What have you been doing?"

He told her a tale of being involved in the King's business, of the obstacles he faced and the little progress he was making. He did not tell her of the attacks on him or how he had moved to the security of the Tower. He did not wish to alarm her, for the fewer people who knew what was going on the better. Moreover, there was something about The Mitre, about the morose giant, Peter, he did not like, a feeling of unease, something he could not express and it troubled him.

Corbett asked Alice what she had been doing but she simply shrugged. "Nothing really," she replied. "I manage the inn, or I try to. The King is due to enter the city very soon and we must prepare for the celebrations. There are pirates in the channel raiding our ships." She smiled at him. "Nothing out of the ordinary, unlike you clerks with your important secret business!"

They sat and teased each other. Corbett ached with a need to gather her in his arms and take her upstairs, anywhere they could be alone, but he knew she would refuse and the presence of the surly Peter dampened his ardour. Instead Corbett made her promise that she would wait for him on the following evening, made his fond farewells and left the tavern, his thick cloak slung over his arm for the weather had turned warm and, if attacked, he would be more free to defend himself and use it as a shield.

When he arrived back in the Tower, he found Ranulf waiting for him, sprawled on his narrow cot. "Yes," he answered Corbett wearily. "I went to Westminster and managed to see Burnell, though that fat pompous Hubert," he added bitterly, "tried to stop me. So, I just stayed outside the Chancellor's chamber shouting your name and that of the King. It worked. Burnell sent for me. He looked at the bible and the drawings you told me to point out, especially the last one." Ranulf paused to sniff and wipe his nose on the sleeve of his jerkin before continuing: "The Chancellor took one look at the last picture and jumped to his feet, yelling for clerks and messengers and demanding that the stables prepare the fleetest horses. He glared at me and I thought I was for the hangman but then he dismissed me with this simple message for you. 'Tell Corbett that I want names.' That's all." Ranulf concluded. Corbett nodded, kicked his boots off and lay on his own cot to ease the bruised aching of his body. Names! The Chancellor wanted

names. Corbett could tell why Duket was murdered and
how, but who? Apart from the apostate priest, and he was
dead, he had no names.

Corbett shivered and pulled his cloak firmly over him, the
metal brooch clasp hit him on the mouth and he sat up to
arrange the cloak better. He looked closer at the brooch,
drawing at the threads caught there until they lay in the
palm of his hand. So tiny, so light, and so insignificant. Yet
Corbett felt the sword pierce his soul and could almost taste
the rank metal at the back of his throat. A series of images
formed in his mind, clearing the doubts and troubles which
had festered there, as when boils or buboes burst, the agony
was intense. He felt a pain in his chest as if a mailed fist was
clenching his heart while the blood pounded and roared in
his ears like breaking surf. He lay down on his cot, his fists
now tightly clenched while he tried to restore order to the
chaos crashing about him. Ranulf came up to him, anxious
and concerned. "Was there anything wrong? Could he fetch
some wine?" Corbett drove him off with a mouthful of foul
abuse and Ranulf, seeing Corbett's white face and wild
staring eyes, simply slunk from the room like a beaten dog.
Neville came in an hour or so later but Corbett just stared
and waved him away. Ranulf did not sleep there that night,
as he preferred the relative safety and security of the
guardroom to the company of his apparently demented
master.

The next morning, however, Ranulf found Corbett up,
washed and dressed, sitting on his cot, writing tray on his
knee, scratching away with his pen on a long piece of
vellum. The clerk still looked pale and drawn. Ranulf began
to make solicitous enquiries but then lapsed into silence
under Corbett's stony gaze. Ranulf knew something terrible
had happened but could not imagine what it could be. His
master was so secretive in all matters that it was difficult to

determine whether he was happy or sad. Ranulf stood, shuffling his feet, until Corbett finished writing, looked up and ordered Ranulf to take the letter to Nigel Couville in the Chancery offices at Westminster. Corbett insisted that the matter was so important that Ranulf was to wait until a reply was ready and bring it straight back to him. Ranulf left immediately, leaving his master to his thoughts and the fresh piece of vellum he had begun writing on.

Ranulf took the boat from the Tower to Westminster and, after making enquiries around the Great Hall, managed to secure an interview with the old keeper of the records. After reading Corbett's note, Couville listened to him attentively. Ranulf could see that he was concerned about Corbett and knew that he had done nothing to resolve the old man's anxieties by describing his master's strange and wild appearance. "Just like he was after his wife and child died," Couville murmured. "Nevertheless," he continued briskly. "Maybe this information will be of use." Ranulf had to stay with Couville for a number of days, fretting and biding his time while the old man searched amongst records and sent his clerks here and there over the city with enquiries or petitions for information. Eventually, after a few days, Couville gave Ranulf a small scroll and ordered him to take it back to Corbett at the Tower. Ranulf immediately complied, glad to be free of Couville's cramped office and the even more restricted quarters the old man had given him.

Ranulf found his master still pale and rather dejected on the parapet above the Tower moat, leaning against the crenellated battlements and staring emptily into the dark waters below. Corbett hardly bothered to greet Ranulf but snatched the document he had brought from Couville and read it greedily, muttering and groaning, almost as if he had expected to find what he read there. He then ordered Ranulf to rest and eat before entrusting him with another short letter to take to Mistress Alice atte Bowe at The Mitre Tavern. Corbett instructed Ranulf, once he delivered the message, to occupy himself in the city and, he added abruptly, if possible, to stay out of trouble. Ranulf immediately departed for the Tower kitchens. Corbett waited until his footsteps faded into the distance and, covering his face with his hands, wept bitterly in a mixture of rage, self-pity and a deep sense of loss.

Seventeen

Three days later Corbett had the Tower cooks put some pastries, sweetmeats and wine into his saddlebag and, after a few words with Swynnerton and Neville, made his way out of the postern gate of the Tower to his meeting with Alice. He had asked to meet her in the fields just outside the north-east corner of the Tower amongst the Roman ruins which criss-crossed the fields with their whitened skeletal walls, the relics of faded ancient glory. Alice was already there, standing by one of the walls, wrapped in a fur-lined cloak which covered the green taffeta dress beneath, her long black hair falling to her shoulders and a red headband decorated with gold stars circling her forehead. Corbett could only secretly marvel at her beauty. He kissed her warmly on the brow and felt her arms melt round his body. He stood there, her dark head on his chest and stared across the ruins. Then he held her at arm's length and teased her about arriving on time. She laughed and flirted back though he noticed her eyes were guarded, wary as if conscious of something wrong. Corbett spread the cleanest blanket he had managed to find and they sat, their backs to one of the ruined walls, while they enjoyed the warmth of a strong spring sun.

They ate and drank, laughed and talked until Alice, almost as if she was a player in some mystery drama, turned and asked how his investigation was proceeding. Corbett sipped the wine from his cup while his other hand rested in Alice's lap. "Duket," he began slowly, "was murdered." He felt no reaction from Alice, so he dug into his purse and pulled out the long silken threads. "Oh, I forgot," he added smilingly, "when you undid the clasp of my cloak these strands got caught in the hook. I think they're from your gloves. I am sorry, I must have ruined them." He dropped the threads into the small black silk-clad palm of her hand.

Alice looked at them and stared at Corbett before bursting into peals of laughter. "You have not brought me here surely," she teased, "to apologize for ruining a glove? I have many others." She leaned across and kissed him gently on the cheek, her lips were like the finest gauze or silk.

Corbett gripped his cup tighter and turned to look into her eyes full of dark laughter. "No," he murmured. "I did not bring you here to talk about silk gloves." He stretched his legs out, relaxed and sighed.

"Duket," Corbett began again, "was a goldsmith and a homosexual, but also a loyal Londoner and a faithful subject of the King. However, his secret longings and dark fantasies led him to Crepyn, a moneylender, a secret admirer of the dead de Montfort and a leader of the banned Populares party here in the city. Crepyn was also a sorcerer, involved in black magic, a member, maybe even the leader of a secret coven which called itself the Pentangle. A group long active in this country, I understand there are similar covens and societies in the East." Corbett felt Alice stiffen beside him as if she was shocked by these revelations.

"How do you know this?" she asked.

Corbett grimaced. "It's not a question of knowing. It is only a guess, a reasoned one, a logical deduction, as my old lecturer in philosophy would say. Anyway," he continued, "another logical deduction is that Crepyn got to know of

Duket's dark secret. He may have seduced him, he certainly seduced Duket's sister. He drew Duket like some helpless fish into his net by pandering to all his needs. You see, he needed Duket for his gold, as he did a number of goldsmiths in the city. With this gold, Crepyn and his party intended to lead a revolt in the city. His coven were as opposed to Edward as they were to our sovereign's ancestors. Some of whom, like William Rufus, they destroyed in the same way they intended to kill our present sovereign lord, with an arrow from an assassin's bow, on the thirty-first of March as the King entered the city from Woodstock, making his way through Newgate and down Cheapside."

"No! Oh, no!" Alice's face was ashen and drawn, her wild eyes staring at him. "Crepyn!" she exclaimed. "An assassin! A regicide!" Corbett glanced at Alice and put his fingers gently on her lips before lightly stroking her cheek.

"Oh, yes," he continued. "Crepyn was an assassin and the arrow was to be shot from the tower of Saint Mary Le Bow, the same church in which our poor goldsmith was hanged. However," he paused to fill his wine goblet. "However, Duket, though he played the part assigned to him, was no assassin. He must have learnt, guessed or deduced what Crepyn and his coven intended to do, although ignorant of the actual details. This is where things went terribly wrong for both of them. On the day of the murder, Duket and Crepyn met in Cheapside. I think Duket became hysterical with fear. Crepyn probably tried to reason with him but Duket drew his dagger and stabbed him through the heart. Duket then panicked. He knew he was in danger so he fled for sanctuary."

"To Saint Mary Le Bow?" Alice interjected.

Corbett nodded. "Yes, of all places, Saint Mary Le Bow, for how was Duket to know, not being a member of Crepyn's inner circle, that Saint Mary Le Bow was one of the

Pentangle's meeting-places and its rector, Roger Bellet, a prominent member of its secret hierarchy? Bellet, of course, gave him sanctuary but immediately contacted the rest of the coven. They decided that Duket had to die as they could not allow him to come to trial and blab everything to get a King's pardon or be released on a plea of self-defence."

Corbett stopped and plucked at the short, fresh spring grass. He looked sideways up at Alice's face but she was sitting rigid with her back against the crumbling wall, gazing out over the fields. "So," he continued, "the coven was alerted and now we come to the two fickle elements in our existence, time and human will. A number of people converged on Saint Mary Le Bow. The first was a boy, Simon, an apprentice during the day, so Ranulf told me, but by night he worked as a tapster and bumboy in a secret drinking place for homosexuals. He probably loved Duket and, when the news of Crepyn's murder and Duket's flight swept through Cheapside, Simon came running. He could not enter the church as there must have been others standing in the entrance so, being of a slight build, he managed to squeeze through one of the windows."

Corbett paused for a short while. "We can only conjecture on what happened next for Simon too is dead, murdered, but I suspect he and Duket moved over to the shadowed recesses of the sanctuary. There, the boy fell asleep while Duket went back to the security of the Blessed Chair. The Watch then arrived. Bellet locked the door from the outside while Duket bolted it from within according to custom. Before the priest left the church, he gave the man in sanctuary the usual meal, a loaf of bread and a jug of wine, and Duket should have stayed there safe and sound until the morning. Of course he did not. He was murdered!"

"Why murder?" Alice interrupted. The question was clipped, her voice terse with tension.

"Oh, that was obvious. Why should Duket commit suicide when he had fled for protection? Why didn't he open his veins? He had a dagger and there were more convenient places to hang himself from besides that iron bar. In fact it was that iron bar which convinced me that he had been murdered."

Alice leaned forward, her hands clasped, resting on her knees. "Why the bar?"

"Oh, it was too high," Corbett replied. "Or rather Duket was too short. You see I measured his corpse, no way could he reach that bar. Then the chair was too clean, almost polished as if the person who had stood on it had been too thorough. Either that or they had rags tied round their boots."

"Rags!" Alice turned her face towards him and Corbett almost jerked back, the laughter had gone from her eyes, only a deep, glittering malice stared back at him.

"Yes, rags," his eyes slid away from her and he felt beneath his cloak for the handle of his dagger. "The murderers wore rags on their boots to muffle any sound."

"Then how did they get in? You said that the church was bolted from inside," Alice snapped.

"Oh, it was but the murderers never got in. They were allowed in sometime in the afternoon before the ward Watch arrived, probably whilst Duket was busy elsewhere in the sanctuary. They came and hid in the shadowed recesses of the entrance. Duket never suspected and, of course, the Watch would never dream of looking there. When it was dark the murderers struck, quietly gliding up the nave, they seized Duket, now drugged by the laced wine given to him by Bellet and, using the Blessed Chair, hanged him before going back to hide in the dark shelter of the doorway. They probably gagged Duket to ensure his silence, hence the strands of cloth caught between his teeth, and pinioned his arms, hence the bruises just above the elbow. The murderers only made one real mistake, they never knew the boy was there and I suspect the coven arrived in the church after he had got through the window and when Duket and the boy were engaged in the far corner of the sanctuary out of their view. Nevertheless, the coven kept a watch and when they saw me meet Simon, they correctly deduced that he must know something and had him killed."

Corbett stopped and glanced at Alice, but still she sat rigid almost ignoring him. "Anyway," he continued, "the next morning the door was forced by the Watch under the supervision of a very garrulous priest who ensured the guards concentrated on poor Duket while the coven simply slipped out into the deserted streets of Cheapside."

Alice turned, both her hands on Corbett's arm, her face alabaster white with a sheen of sweat on her brow. "But the murderers?" she asked, "Who are they?"

Corbett moved a wisp of hair from her forehead which had escaped from her headband and ran his fingers down the side of her face. "The boy Simon," he murmured, "before he was killed said that he saw two of the figures. A giant and a dwarf. You see, the murderers didn't know that he was there." Corbett looked directly at Alice. "The giant was Peter, Alice, you know that. He was there, he fastened the noose like the hangman he is, professionally, tying the knot under Duket's left ear. Duket did not do that. A goldsmith about to commit suicide would never have done that. You know that Peter was there, Alice, because you were there with him!"

He touched Alice's hand and felt the ice of her skin. "You, small, cloaked and hooded, were what Simon called 'the dwarf'. You would be, beside Peter. I thought the same when I saw you last at The Mitre. I thought there was something strange when you called Ranulf my bodyguard but Ranulf was never introduced as that. He left The Mitre as soon as he saw Peter. So, Alice, how did you know?"

Alice turned her back on him, head bowed, her hands clenched. "You are still guessing, Master Clerk," she murmured. "You have no proof, no evidence that I was there."

"Oh, yes, I have," Corbett answered. "Or rather you now have it!" Alice whirled round, her eyes dilated with fury and rage, the skin of her face stretched like gauze across her cheekbones. She looked older, wilder, her lips drawn back almost curled with anger but Corbett simply stared at her. "I gave it to you," he said, "the black silk threads!"

"But they were caught on the clasp of your brooch!" Alice almost shrieked at him.

"No," Corbett dug into his wallet and drew out more black silk threads. "These are the ones caught on my brooch. The threads you have were taken from the rope tied round Duket's neck."

Alice now knelt on the ground, her gown billowing round her like a cloak. Only her face, small, white and naked, betrayed a mixture of anger and terror. She raised her arms and slowly removed the gloves from her hands as if peeling an apple. She put them down and stretched out her hands, palms up. "You know about these?" she asked.

Corbett looked at the small, bright purple inverted cross on her palms which looked like brand marks recently burnt on. "Yes," he answered. "The marks of Fitz-Osbert. I guessed you had them but Couville ... " he looked at her. "You will not know him but he conducted a search of letters, charters and writs and drew up a report. You wish to read it?"

Alice shook her head. "Why should I?" she replied. "I know its contents better than you. I was married to Thomas atte Bowe, vintner of Cheapside, but I was born in

Southwark. My maiden name was Dachert but, secretly, I always called myself Alice Fitz-Osbert, my mother's name. She had the marks as I had. She told me about our family, the persecution of our great ancestor, William Fitz-Osbert, and others by the House of Plantagenet. The Fitz-Osberts, my uncles and cousins, were ardent supporters of de Montfort and fought with him to the very end, dying with him in the slaughter at Evesham." Alice traced the mark on her right hand. "From the beginning I was initiated into these mysteries and got to know and love the Lord Lucifer! I used my wealth to blend the Fitz-Osbert hatred for the Plantagenets with that of the followers of de Montfort and others of the Populares party. I built up the Pentangle, an intimate, close organization which worked together, though the identity of each individual was known only to me. I am 'The Hooded One', only you and one other know that, the rest thought I was a man. I plotted against the Plantagenet, destroyed his spy, spread dissension and was responsible for Duket's death. All for a dream and a reality you could not begin to understand."

"Nonsense!" Corbett shouted and got to his feet. "Incantations, spells, dancing in circles, heathen rites and now treason. Is it worth being hung in chains above a fire at Smithfield?" He glared at Alice. "That," he almost spat the words out, "is the punishment for sorcerers and traitors!"

Alice smoothed the creases on the front of her dress, her hands fluttering like small white birds hovering over a dark green field. She looked up at Corbett and he realized that she was calmer, the colour had returned to her face, but the light and laughter had gone from her eyes. "Your religion," she replied, "may matter to you, mine certainly does to me. It is older than Christianity, was practised here even before the Romans came, but the church has driven it underground."

"Then why the treason?" Corbett asked.

Alice shrugged. "King Edward has to die. He has smashed the Welsh and done great damage to the old religion, its shrines and graves in the west just like he did in Palestine. He was hated for killing de Montfort and crushing the Populares movement here in London! He deserves to die! He would have done, when he entered the city. Master bowmen, stationed on the tower of Saint Mary Le Bow, would have brought him down. Then we would have seized our arms stored around that church and risen in rebellion."

Alice almost smiled. "We nearly succeeded but for Duket and his foolish murder of Crepyn. It was not that we mourned Crepyn though he was one of us, but more that Duket had to be killed. We know he suspected our true aims and might have bartered this knowledge for a pardon for Crepyn's death. Perhaps he deliberately chose Saint Mary Le Bow to draw the attention of the government. Bellet was a member of the Pentangle, his cemetery held stores of arms. Savel, the royal spy, discovered that and died. So we could not let Duket live. He threatened us all!"

"And me?" Corbett asked.

Alice's eyes slid away from his. "I don't really know." Her voice was so low that he could hardly hear it. "As the Pentangle, indeed, as The Hooded One, I wanted you dead but, as an individual, I was anxious about the sentence passed and, so, so relieved to see you always walk away unscathed. The Pentangle, not I, decided that you must die. Twice, we tried in Thames Street, then we waited for you outside Saint Katherine's but the boy was early, he died and his corpse drew a crowd. When Bellet was arrested, we knew you would go to his house. But each time you were saved. We thought you had a charmed life and wished that you were one of us."

"You are lying!" Corbett was almost shouting. "Somebody gave you information about where I was and what I was doing! Who was it?"

Alice beckoned with her hand and, when Corbett drew close, quietly murmured a few words into his ear. Corbett stared at her, smiled coldly and drew away. She could have told him outright but, getting close to her, he felt her soft lips near his face, smelt the perfume of her hair and body and realized he could still lose his soul in such a soft deadly trap.

Corbett shook his head and scuffed at the grass with the toe of his boot.

"Is the rest as I described?" he asked.

"Yes," Alice smiled tightly, like a little girl admitting she was wrong when caught out in mischief.

"And the others?" he queried.

She looked at him sharply, the smile had gone. "Your King will have to hunt them down, Master Clerk," she snapped.

"That will be easy. They are not far away," Corbett murmured. "There are those at The Mitre, one will break."

"And me? I am not afraid to die," Alice whispered.

Corbett looked into her dark eyes and saw the terror there; she was lying and he knew that she was asking for pity. He crouched down and cupped her face in his hands. "I can do little for you, Alice," he said gently. "I cannot get you a pardon, not for this. I cannot ignore you as some others may well use your name to buy mercy. You cannot hide for the rest of your life for, if you did, they would surely hunt you down." He stopped talking and kissed her gently on her eyelids, tasting her tears. She was a murderess, a sorcerer and traitor but his love cut through such names.

"Listen, Alice," he continued quickly, "tomorrow I will write my report for Burnell. The day after I will send it to him. That is the day he will strike, The Mitre will be surrounded. You must flee today. You must not inform the others. They are lost and," he lied, "already under scrutiny.

Do you understand?" She nodded and he kissed her on the brow, smelling the faint fragrance of her hair.

Corbett rose and walked quickly away. He thought he heard her call his name but he did not turn back and dismissed it as the screech of a gull hunting in the mudflats along the river bank.

Eighteen

True to his word, Corbett spent the following day drawing up his report for Burnell, hoping that Alice would save herself and not warn the rest of her coven. Ranulf was still absent so Corbett asked Swynnerton to send one of his more intelligent squires into the city to see if anything untoward was happening in The Mitre. The squire returned late in the evening, quite drunk, but after Corbett had doused him in a tub of icy moat water, he recovered sufficiently to report that he had noticed nothing extraordinary.

Early the next morning Corbett finished his report; it contained all that he had told Alice with a few additional facts and observations. He re-read it then, satisfied, sanded and sealed it 'for the Chancellor only', and sent it into the city under an armed escort from the Tower. The task done, he wandered out of the Tower back to the place he had met Alice a few days before. The grass where they had sat still bore the scuff marks of their boots and the silence and lonely desolation of the ruins a marked contrast to the passion and fury he had felt when he had first visited the place. He was about to turn away when he saw a posy of spring flowers resting on the top of the wall, tied in a bunch by a small black silk glove. Alice had left them, knowing he would return. Corbett picked them up and slipped the flowers inside his jerkin and sat slumped against the wall, cursing his luck, preferring anything rather than face the yawning emptiness in his heart.

Corbett stared across the fields and realized that he had one more task to accomplish. He hurriedly went back to the Tower and left hasty instructions for Swynnerton and Ranulf. From a cleric in the Tower he borrowed a thick, heavy, brown cloak with a cowl to cover his head, rubbed crushed ash into his hair and face and, disguised in both dress and behaviour like an old monk, left the Tower and took a barge to Westminster. He arrived at the usual place but, when he had slowly climbed the steps from the river, he ignored the usual route to the Great Hall and made his way instead to the main entrance of the abbey. Inside he ambled slowly up the great nave of the church not bothering to stare at the pure spotless white walls, the trellised stonework or the soaring majesty of the pillars which seemed to make the roof of the church float on air as if by magic.

Despite the thin sunlight streaking through the coloured windows, the abbey was dark and Corbett felt protected in his disguise. He knew his way around the abbey and slipped through a side entrance into the deserted cloisters where only an old monk sat on the low brick wall. The old man gaped with rheumy eyes and drooling mouth at Corbett, raising a skeletal hand in doubtful salute. Corbett nodded in return and walked on, forcing himself to keep to a slow shuffle, head bowed, hands concealed in the thick bell-like sleeves of the cloak. He looked around the cloisters, but they were empty except for the old monk and a raven which stalked across the ground, its cruel yellow beak jabbing at the thin sparse grass. Corbett continued on to the south-east corner of the cloisters, and sat down on the low wall, his head bowed as if in silent prayer, whilst his hands searched desperately at the stonework below him. Eventually he found it, a loose brick which could be slid in or out. Corbett pretended to drop something and crouched down to look for it. He found the brick was completely free of plaster and, when withdrawn, left a small gap.

Corbett slid his hand in but found nothing, breathed slowly to hide his excitement and almost screamed aloud as someone tapped him on the shoulder. He whirled round, his hand going beneath his cloak for the dagger but it was only the old monk, his drooling lips parted in a toothless smile, his vacant eyes searching for companionship. Corbett hastily sketched a *Benedicte* and the old man bowed and shuffled off mumbling to himself. Corbett watched him go, rose and glanced furtively around. There was still no one about. Had he come too late for that particular day? He decided to stay and, climbing over the low wall, made his way to the far corners of the cloisters and a weed filled clump of bushes. He pushed through them, ignoring the cold, wet, overgrown leaves and the water which soaked his gown with its icy droplets. Corbett concealed himself, certain he was hidden from view and so began his vigil.

The cloisters remained deserted, the monks of the abbey were either in the scriptorium or involved in their various tasks. The old monk wandered back for a while and others also passed; servants, domestics and officers of the abbey but none stayed. It was too cold and Corbett wondered how long he could stay; his legs and feet were now freezing, the cold gripping his body like an icy mailed fist. The bells of the abbey were beginning to toll for early evening prayer when a cowled figure suddenly entered the cloisters and walked quickly to the same spot where Corbett had sat earlier. After looking around, the stranger stopped to remove the brick and searched the gap. The figure then straightened and hastily walked back the way he had come. Hugh had not been able to glimpse the face hidden deep in the cowl so he waited until the man left the cloisters before following in pursuit.

Corbett re-entered the now darkening abbey and saw the figure ahead of him skulking across the nave towards a small door in the north wall, and, without looking around, disappeared through a half-open door. He stopped to regain his breath before following, turned and realized that he was in a deserted area which stretched between the abbey and the palace, strewn with scaffolding and brick kilns left by workmen putting finishing touches to the outside wall on the abbey's north side. He sensed that his quarry might escape in the gathering dusk and so strode silently but swiftly towards him. The figure, alarmed by some sound, was half turning as Corbett grasped him tightly by the shoulder. The man shrugged off Corbett's hand and backed away.

"What is it? What do you want?" The voice was slightly fearful.

Corbett pulled back his own cowl to reveal his identity. "Why, Master Hubert Seagrave," he said. "It is only Hugh Corbett. I thought I recognized your voice." Corbett peered closer. "It is Master Hubert of the Chancery is it not?" A pair of soft, plump, white hands pulled back the cowl and Hubert, prim-lipped and cold-eyed, stared back at Corbett.

"Master Corbett," he murmured. "Why are you floundering around in the dusk?" Hubert rolled his eyes coyly like some innocent maid. "Did you think that I was someone else?"

"Where have you been?" Corbett snapped.

"At my prayers. Why, what business is it of yours?"

"Prayers!" Corbett felt the rage pounding in his head. "No prayers, Master Hubert. I doubt you ever pray. You have just been to see if your friends in the Pentangle have left you any money or a message. You are a traitor, Master Hubert, and I shall prove that!"

Hubert narrowed his eyes speculatively and Corbett

sensed that his opponent, beneath his puppy fat and the elegant mannerisms of a court clerk, was a very dangerous man.

"You have no proof, Master Corbett," Hubert said mockingly.

"You did not even ask who the Pentangle is," Corbett bitingly interrupted. "In fact you may be one of them."

"No," Hubert shrieked in a high-pitched voice. "Not the Pentangle, Corbett, but the Populares, yes. The people's party. My father fought and died at Evesham, my uncles and cousins at other battles, while those who were left adorned the gibbets around London." Hubert stopped speaking, his eyes glaring at Corbett, his mouth half open in rage as he struggled to control himself. He leaned against a brick kiln.

"You have no proof, Master Corbett," he said again.

Corbett smiled and shook his head. "Oh, yes I do. I know The Hooded One. I know who she is. She has told me that you were the Pentangle's spy in the Chancery but I had to catch you red-handed!"

"She!" Hubert whispered hoarsely.

"Never mind that," Corbett jibed. "You told them about me. You told Bellet when I was going to the church of Saint Mary Le Bow. You told the assassins where I lived and what time I returned. Above all, you told them about my past life, about my dead wife and young child, about my love of the flute. You gathered information, you collected it like some rat scurrying around the Chancery collects bits of wax, anything to chew on, information to be sold at a profit. I can prove this. After all, there are not many clerks in the Chancery. I suspect that the King's torturers will begin with you!"

Corbett leaned closer and watched the fear start in Hubert's eyes. "The Pentangle is finished," he whispered. "And so are the Populares. Probably while you are out looking to see if your masters left money for information received, the Chancellor is already issuing orders for the arrest of people all over the city. You may be one of them! You are betrayed, Hubert, by no less a person than The Hooded One. She told me where and when the Pentangle's spy in the Chancery left his information. I would tell you her name but what does it matter, I am going to see you die!''

Hubert gnawed at his lips with fear and looked anxiously around.

"I can give you gold," he replied huskily. "Look!" He opened his cloak and Corbett thought he was scrabbling for his purse but jumped back when he saw the faint glint of steel and Hubert drew the sword he had hidden there.

Corbett now knew that his adversary was no longer the soft, effete clerk for Hubert held his sword like any trained soldier or street fighter. He advanced towards Corbett, the cruel point of his sword not wavering. Corbett hastily drew his own long Welsh dagger, stepping back carefully searching for a foothold, and all the time watching Hubert's face.

"Master Corbett," Hubert snapped. "I am going to kill you and then I will disappear.'

Corbett was about to reply when he realized his mistake for Hubert suddenly lunged towards him, the sword's point searching for his heart. He struggled backwards, his feet hit some wood and he crashed on his back on the ground. Hubert stood between his legs and laid the sword point to Corbett's throat, gently pushing until Corbett felt a pinprick of pain and a faint trickle of blood.

"Well, Corbett?" Hubert cocked his head to one side as if meditating on what to do next. Corbett's fingers were flailing, searching on the ground where he lay. There was nothing. He grasped what he thought was some sand and, as Hubert brought the sword back, flung it into the man's face, while he rolled to one side.

Hubert fell to his knees, screaming with pain. "I am blind! I am blind!" he shrieked. Corbett smelt his own hand and realized that he had thrown lime straight into his opponent's face. He picked up Hubert's fallen sword and, without a flicker of remorse, brought it down in one sweeping curve to bite deep into Hubert's neck. A great fountain of blood spurted out and with a long sigh the body simply toppled to one side and lay still. Corbett felt no regrets or sorrow at what he had done. He wiped the bloody sword on his dead enemy's cloak and carefully searched around the ground. Eventually, near the place he had fallen, he found the lime pit and, dragging Hubert's corpse by the heels, pulled him to the side and pushed him gently in. The body bobbed for a while on the surface before slowly sinking from view.

Nineteen

Corbett arrived back in the Tower late in the evening to find Sir Edward Swynnerton frenetic and the Tower abustle with activity as if expecting attack. Sir Edward, Neville beside him, was ordering horses out and rooms refurbished. Ranulf was sitting against a wall, staring like a gargoyle, mouth open, face twisted with concern. Corbett called over to him and Ranulf's face broke into a cheery grin as he ambled over to join his master. "Well, Ranulf," Corbett said, more pleased than he had expected to see his assistant back again. "You enjoyed the city?"

"Yes," Ranulf replied. "I went back to Thames Street to check on our lodgings."

"And all was safe?" Corbett interrupted.

"As secure as the Tower itself," Ranulf answered. He did not dare tell his master about his seduction of Mistress Grant, a fine lady, Ranulf mused, with her silken plump thighs and small rounded breasts. She went down like a drawbridge, Ranulf thought, all squeals and protests but obliging all the same.

Corbett watched him suspiciously. There was something wrong though he decided it would have to wait, for he caught sight of Swynnerton out of the corner of his eyes, huffing and puffing his way across to him.

"It must be you, Master Clerk," he barked.

"I beg your pardon?" Corbett said.

"It must be you," Swynnerton pressed home the point. "The city is full of soldiers and not just country bumpkins collected by Commissioners of Array but professional veterans, mercenaries hired by the King and usually kept at a far distance from the city." The old soldier paused for breath before continuing: "They are going to be sent here. I also understand the King has summoned the Mayor and Aldermen to Woodstock and has issued writs to sheriffs ordering a levy of men in the shires. The ports are to be closed and ... "

"And you think it is all because of me?" Corbett abruptly interrupted. Swynnerton edged closer and Corbett smelt his stale breath. "Master Clerk, I know it is because of you. You're a very dangerous man, aren't you? You were right about that priest and God knows what else you have uncovered! I'll be glad when you're gone!" Swynnerton then dug beneath his cloak and drew out a sealed letter. "This arrived for you." He dropped the writ into Corbett's hand and walked away.

Corbett studied the personal seal of the Lord Chancellor and carefully opened the letter. It was fulsome. Burnell thanked Corbett, 'his dear and trusted clerk for his work in bringing to light the evil conspiracy which had flourished like a canker in the fairest city of the King's realm'. He then bluntly continued that Corbett was to proceed immediately to the royal palace of Woodstock outside Oxford to receive thanks from a grateful monarch.

Corbett sighed, folded the letter and put it into his pouch. On any other occasion Corbett would have been delighted with such an order for a personal meeting with the King meant preferment and patronage in the arduous climb to high office. Nevertheless, Corbett reasoned, he would be glad to be free of London and the Tower whilst the hunt for the conspirators took place. He thought of Alice and anxiously wondered if she had escaped. He turned and walked back to his lodgings, his anxieties and worries gnawing at his soul, threatening to drown it in a fit of black depression. He had to move, keep actively involved in affairs, anything rather than be drawn into the savage whirlpool of regret and desperation.

Within hours Corbett had organized Ranulf into obtaining two horses and a sumpter pony, on which all their baggage was piled and securely tied. Ranulf was so pleased to be going, to be leaving London where there seemed so much danger, for Ranulf had reached the private conclusion that it was safer to be a criminal or felon than be an officer of the law. In addition, as he proudly proclaimed to anyone who bothered to listen, this was the first time he had been out of the city. In his turn, Swynnerton was only too pleased to see the back of Corbett, who had severely upset the harmony of life and routine at the Tower, and eagerly supplied the enigmatic clerk with the necessary documents to get out of the city and travel to Oxford.

Just before dark, Corbett and Ranulf bade their farewell to the garrison, led their horses through the postern gate and began their journey north. Corbett knew he would have to lodge at a tavern but he was determined to be out of the city as quickly as possible. At first, Ranulf was excited and talkative but his master's clipped answers, guarded looks and the sheer fascination of travel silenced him and he hung back a little, busily looking around him and trying to control the sumpter pony which seemed to have taken a savage dislike to him. Since they had left the Tower, which lay outside the city wall, they were free of interference from city officials, though the roads to and from London were being well patrolled and they eventually met a group of soldiers under a serjeant-of-arms.

They were the same hardened professionals Swynnerton had mentioned the King was sending into the city: Corbett had served with such men in Wales and along the Welsh March. Hard-faced, their skin toughened and burnt by the sun and wind, hair closely cropped to make their helmets and caps easier to wear. They were stationed at a bridge that Corbett had to cross and quietly surrounded him and Ranulf. Their leader inspected Swynnerton's letters and warrants while the rest of the escort checked the horses and casually prodded bundles strapped on the sumpter pony whose wicked temperament ensured this was done with the greatest care.

After a few questions, they were allowed to cross and continue their journey into the gathering darkness until Corbett decided to stay at a roadside tavern whose ale-bush, welcoming light and hot food were a welcome relief, despite the dirty rushes, ale-stained tables and the offensive smell of tallow candles and animal fat. Once again, they ran into a party of soldiers who were also staying there. The same questions were asked and the same answers given, before Corbett and Ranulf were left alone to their steaming bowls of soup and makeshift beds on the flea-ridden floor.

So, their journey continued for four days. Sometimes they joined groups of other travellers; merchants, hawkers and pedlars, the occasional lawyer going up to the Halls of Oxford or groups of loud-mouthed students in their long patched robes returning to their studies. Corbett and Ranulf engaged in desultory conversation with these companions and all reported an increase in military traffic on the London roads.

There was constant speculation on the reason why, though most welcomed it, for, despite the King's ordinances to cut back the hedgerows and keep the highways clear and well patrolled, outlaw attacks were common.

Corbett wished to avoid company but Ranulf clearly relished every encounter, particularly the ladies in their ornate litters slung between two horses. Corbett had to intervene occasionally to ensure his servant, as he described Ranulf, did not give offence and provoke the wrath of the accompanying menfolk.

When they were alone, their journey was pleasant enough through woods and copses of oak, juniper, box and beechwood. Sometimes the trees were so crowded together that their spring-freshened branches formed an intricate canopy above their heads, blocking out the weak sunshine. Only then did Ranulf fall silent, afraid of the forest, the eerie darkness beyond the trees, so different from the streets and alleyways of the city.

Corbett, however, felt at home, for such scenes took him back to the heavy dark woods of West Sussex and the even more dangerous ones in Shropshire and along the Welsh March. At other times, as they crossed or went through the clear fertile valleys of the Cotswolds, they passed villages surrounded by their patchwork of fields. The cottages of the villeins, simple oblong buildings with a loft above and a shed or kitchen behind, sometimes dominated by the walled, square-shaped manor house of the lord or bailiff.

Corbett would ignore such sights but Ranulf gawked at the space and openness of such dwellings, loudly comparing them to the rat-infested runnels of the city. At any other time Corbett would have snapped at Ranulf and urged him on, but he began to find the young man's obvious delight in his changing surroundings a pleasant diversion from brooding on his anxieties about Alice.

Corbett also realized that Ranulf had never seen the countryside at work and began to point out the common meadow where the villagers' cattle stood and the pigs rooting at the edge of a copse or wood. Once he stopped to explain and describe a field being ploughed, oxen pulling a two-wheeled heavy plough guided by a man who ensured the heavy-bladed coulter cut straight and deep. Behind him a man walked with a heavy bag slung round his neck from which he scattered seed into the freshly cut furrow, while young boys dispersed the voracious, diving crows with well-armed shots from their slings. Corbett realized that Ranulf understood very little of what he said but was moved by the intensity of his companion's childlike curiosity.

Eventually, the countryside flattened out and they moved closer to the river on their approach to Oxford. Corbett had to patiently explain to Ranulf that London was not the only city in the kingdom, a fact Ranulf soon absorbed when he approached the town gates and, skirting the threatening castle, entered the city itself. It had been years since Corbett had been in Oxford but little appeared to have changed. The place was thronged with scholars, students, portly officials and learned lecturers, specialists in Theology, Philosophy, Logic and the Scriptures.

Corbett decided to stay at New Hall and obtained, without much difficulty, a sparse whitewashed cell for himself and Ranulf with stabling for his horses at a nearby inn. Corbett, to Ranulf's astonishment, immediately asked for a tub in the Hall's wash-house to be filled with hot water and, when it was ready, stripped and immersed himself in it washing away the grime and dirt of his stay at the Tower and the journey to Oxford. He then insisted that the terrified Ranulf follow suit and by the time Ranulf had finished, the water was as black as charcoal. Corbett ordered the tub emptied, refilled and put the hapless Ranulf, who stood shivering wrapped in a robe, back into the water to finish the task as well as wash some clothes which Corbett flung at him before walking out to visit the Hall library.

After a while, Ranulf, clean and scrubbed, joined him

there and Corbett took him round, trying to mollify his companion's evident humiliation and anger at the enforced bathing by showing him the reading carrels and hundred precious books that the library boasted. Each of these was beautifully bound in the softest vellum, chained and padlocked to its stand. Corbett explained the value of each book and the precious care the Hall took over them, hence the warning written on each of their covers. "Wash, lest any touch of dirty finger, on these spotless pages linger."

Corbett then took him from the chapel where the library was housed to the large vaulted Hall for a simple dinner before returning to the sparseness of their cell to sleep and prepare for the following day's journey to Woodstock. By his snores, Corbett knew that Ranulf was soon asleep and could only envy his companion's carefree attitude while he tossed on his narrow cot agitated with anxiety about Alice, remembering the patrols he had encountered travelling to Oxford, going over, time and again, the evidence he had collected and built up against her and her coven. He was still torn between his love for her and his sense of duty to his task and was trying to resolve the dilemma when he fell into an uneasy dream about Alice, Burnell, the sardonic Bellet, the crackling fires of Smithfield and the gibbet at The Elms, tall stark and black against the sky.

Just after dawn Ranulf shook him awake. He rose, splashed cold water over his face from the brass ewer fixed on the wooden stand of the laver and hurriedly dressed in his best robes brought for the occasion. Corbett inspected a neatly turned out Ranulf, grunted that he was satisfied and they then went down to the Hall's kitchen and buttery to break their fast on ale and rye bread.

Their journey to Woodstock was uneventful; skirting the village, they followed the broad beaten track through a large man-made park to the royal palace of Woodstock. It was the first time that Corbett had been there and he was surprised to find it was no more than an enlarged manor house spilling over the brow of a small hill. The principal building was the main hall whose turret, clear against the skyline, stood over the other buildings, offices and chapels which had been later added to it. The building work had gone beyond the old wall and a new, crenellated curtain wall was in the process of just being completed. The place was almost frenetic with activity; carts full of produce fought their way from the main gate. Courtiers in silken clothes and ermine-topped cloaks strolled arm-in-arm, arrogantly surveying all the coming and going. Officials and clerks, messengers of the Court hurried along rapt in their own smug self-importance, while all around the parkland were the bivouacked knights and soldiers of the royal household and other noble retinues.

Cursing and protesting, Corbett led Ranulf through the crowds to the main gate, the most effective aid being the evil-tempered sumpter pony whose sharp teeth and flailing hooves proved remarkably persuasive. At the huge gate, men-at-arms, spears crossed, blocked the entrance and, beyond, a group of knight bannerets from the royal household stood about in half-armour, swords drawn while Corbett had already noted the royal archers patrolling the parapets above him. Corbett had to use the combined warrants of Burnell and Swynnerton to gain entrance to the inner ward where his horses and any arms he and Ranulf carried were deftly taken away from them before one of the household knights reluctantly agreed to send a servant to look for the steward of the royal household. The latter eventually arrived, huffing and puffing with haste. A small, bald, overdressed man with his chest thrust out so that he waddled into view like some portly pigeon. He introduced himself as Walter Boudon and his little pebble eyes gleamed with recognition when Corbett introduced himself.

"Come!" Boudon snapped his fingers.

"Where to?" Corbett asked.

"The King! The King!" Boudon looked surprised. "That is why you have come? Is it not?" His round smooth face wrinkled in astonishment, lips pursed with annoyance. "His Highness is waiting for you," he stuttered, "you must follow me." He turned and waddled off with Corbett and Ranulf in hot pursuit.

Corbett was surprised, for he knew the routine of court and the royal household and had expected to be kept waiting for days.

Boudon led them through a maze of small alleyways, up some steps, through a buttery, kitchen, a small chapel, then up another staircase into the Great Hall of the manor, long and spacious, with a high vaulted timber roof which soared up and over them. The room was unique with its dark red fire-glazed tiles and the large trefoiled window through which the morning sun shone down on a large oaken table on the dais at the far end. Ranulf gawked and even Corbett was astonished at the hall's luxury. The walls were covered in woollen and velvet drapes, whilst costly and richly decorated carpets covered the floor. Aumbries or cupboards with beautiful wrought-iron scroll work on their boarded doors stood in corners and niches. Against the left wall was a large chimney piece with logs spluttering in the grate while before it, seated in large, elaborately carved chairs, sat a man and a woman, both wrapped in furs, leaning across the table between them quietly studying a chess-board.

Boudon muttered to Corbett and Ranulf to stay while he slowly moved across the room and, head bowed, respectfully whispered to the seated man, turning his fat body slightly to indicate Corbett and Ranulf. The man moved a chess-piece and, looking direct at Corbett, called out.

"Master Clerk, come nearer. It's cold and I do not intend to move from this chair. Boudon," he turned to the little fat steward. "Bring some mulled wine."

Corbett and Ranulf walked over and sank to one knee before the table, Ranulf only doing so at Corbett's sudden insistence for the clerk recognized the harsh, imperious voice of the King which he had last heard in that lonely, snow-swept valley so many years before. Corbett introduced himself and Ranulf.

"Yes, yes, Master Clerk." The voice had a slight testy edge. "We know who you are." He clapped his hands and servants appeared as if from nowhere with stools on which Corbett and Ranulf were told to sit. Corbett did so, feeling faintly ridiculous as these seats were low, forcing him to look up into the King's face while trying to fend off the wet nose and slobbery mouth of a large, curious wolfhound which disdainfully walked off when a royal foot swung out to kick him.

The King was simply dressed in a blue cotta which stretched down to black leather boots, over this cotta was a surcoat with capuchon attached and lined with costly ermine around the neck and long sleeves. The only distinguishing marks of royalty were a simple chaplet of gold around his brows and thick gold bands on his wrists. The King studied Corbett carefully and the clerk looked back, noting the grey strands in the straw-coloured hair and close-cut beard which framed the King's long thin lips.

Edward had aged since Wales yet the eyes were still as striking and the large fleshy nose still made the King look like one of his haughty hunting falcons. Edward watched Corbett closely then grinned and leaned across to tap him on the shoulder. "I remember you, Master Corbett, from Wales. It seems we are in debt to you once again for saving our life. I read the Chancellor's letters." He paused to clear his throat. "A memorable feat of deduction!" The King turned as his companion asked a question, her broad nasal tones giving the Norman French a curious ringing twang. Edward replied softly and Corbett bowed as Edward introduced his Queen, the beloved Eleanor of Castile.

Eleanor was a dark-haired, Spanish beauty, her olive skin and delicate sensitive features enhanced by a lacy white wimple which covered her head and framed her slim face. A blue, gold-brocaded dress with a silver chain round the waist and fringed with Bruges lace at the neck and cuffs adorned a body which, Corbett knew, had captivated the King since his engagement to her over thirty years ago. Despite her sensitive face, Corbett knew that Eleanor, so infatuated with her husband, had followed him on crusade as well as his wars in Gascony and Wales. She had borne the King children but, until this year, no male child had survived. Yet her hold over Edward was complete. Even the costly furnishings in this room would be her work for Eleanor had a reputation for being both virtuous and luxury-loving.

When the King finished talking, Eleanor turned, her face radiant with happiness, and extended a slim be-ringed hand for Corbett to kiss. The clerk did so, realizing that anyone responsible for saving the King's life would have Eleanor's complete protection and gratitude. He smelt the faint fragrant perfume of the Queen, immediately thought of Alice and felt a momentary stab of anger at what both these royal personages had cost him.

He looked up in astonishment as the Queen burst into peals of laughter, her hand pointing beyond him to where Ranulf sat. Corbett turned and almost laughed himself at the young man's white face, his wide eyes and slack jaw revealing his awe and trepidation at being in the royal presence. Corbett touched him reassuringly on the knee while the King talked to Ranulf in English which almost parodied the voice of a Londoner. Ranulf stammered a short reply then lapsed into silence, head bowed, as the King summoned Boudon and asked his steward to pour the wine that the servants had eventually brought. Only then Corbett was questioned carefully on all he had discovered in connection with Duket's mysterious death.

Twenty

The King listened to Corbett carefully, now and again interrupting to ask a question or make him repeat a statement to clarify a point. Occasionally, the Queen broke into the conversation with a blunt question or stark observation. Time passed, more wine was brought, this time with sweetmeats which clogged Corbett's mouth and made him feel slightly nauseous. Eventually, Corbett's story ended, he had circumvented Alice, telling slight lies to soften her participation in the plot against the King. Nevertheless, he was uncertain whether the King was ignorant of the full facts. He seemed well briefed, his shrewd eyes assessing Corbett seemed to sense that something was missing. Yet, he appeared pleased and, when Corbett had finished, there was silence as the King stared into the fire, one hand stretched across the table to caress his wife. He got up, his huge bulk towering above Corbett.

"You have done well, Master Clerk," he rasped. "Very well. I shall not forget. Take this," and he dropped two full purses into Corbett's lap "as a mere token of our gratitude. There will be more," he added softly, looking at both Corbett and Ranulf. "But that will come later." The King tapped Corbett on the shoulder. "Enjoy yourself here, Master Clerk. You are a loyal, faithful servant of the Crown who has chosen the better part. Whatever you may think now." Then he was gone, his wife following in a billow of

silk and perfume almost before Corbett and Ranulf could
rise to their feet.

Corbett sat and thought about what he had said to the
King. He sighed, turned and grinned at the still awestruck
Ranulf. "Come, Ranulf," he joked. "The King has told us to
enjoy ourselves. Let us begin."

Corbett stayed at Woodstock for over a week, enjoying
and participating in the ritual and festivities of the Court as
it celebrated Easter and the ending of Holy Week. Gradually
Ranulf relaxed and a cynical Corbett watched him flirt in his
open, vulgar way with the ladies of the Court. The young
man's blatant sexuality and infatuation with the opposite
sex both fascinated and repelled Corbett. The sophisticated
court ladies thought differently, a few of whom found
themselves in Ranulf's bed, turning and working to pleasure
a young man who, by rights, should have been dangling on
the gallows weeks ago.

The days passed. Corbett felt the frantic routine of the
Court soothe his anxieties and regrets about Alice though
the scraps of news from London were ominous enough.
There had been raids on houses both in the city and the
surrounding countryside, arrests had been made, followed
by summary trials before the King's Justices and then brutal
executions at the gallows or in chains at Smithfield. The
King, for all his calm demeanour, was secretly furious at
being kept from his city by rebels, secret sympathizers of the
dead but still hated de Montfort.

Corbett would have stayed at Woodstock immersed in the
Court routine carrying out minor tasks assigned to him by
the King but, of course, Burnell changed all that. About ten
days after arriving at Woodstock, Corbett received a letter
from the Chancellor, and he opened it with trembling
hands, recognizing the bold firm script of the Chancellor's
own hand.

"Robert Burnell, Bishop of Bath and Wells, Chancellor of England, to our well beloved clerk, Hugh Corbett, greetings. The information you sent us has proved most valuable in the apprehension and arrest of traitors in the city. The tavern known as The Mitre in St. Mark's Lane was surrounded by soldiers the King had sent into the city. All persons in that tavern were arrested and taken to the Tower for questioning. There was, however, no sign of the owner, the woman known as Alice atte Bowe. Nevertheless, others were not so fortunate in their escape and once confined in the Tower were put to the question and interrogated for days regarding the murder of Lawrence Duket. A number of them died under this questioning but one, a huge fellow, the protector of Alice atte Bowe and former public hangman called Peter, eventually made a full confession. It would appear that the revolutionaries or Populares party in the city, those known supporters of the dead de Montfort, were infiltrated and controlled by an even more dangerous faction, a secret black magic coven called the Pentangle.

"This group rejected the cross of Christ and saw the heretic, Fitz-Osbert, as a saint espousing theories which would have done away with the authority of the King, the church and any vestige of authority in this realm. They practised Satanic ceremonies and abominable rites in deserted churchyards or, more commonly, in the chancel of a disused church in Southwark. The leader of this group, known as The Hooded One, was, Peter abjectly confessed, the woman, Alice atte Bowe, who owned The Mitre tavern. Some others in the group were wealthy merchants, even officials in the city government. One of them, Ralph Crepyn, had the specific task to raise money, by whatever means he could employ, to assist the Pentangle and the Populares party in the city with their plot to kill the King, as his Grace moved from Woodstock through Cheapside and down to Westminster.

"The King's murder was to be followed by a general revolt. The drawing you found in Bellet's bible showed that the assassins would have used the church of Saint Mary Le Bow, the same place they used

*to store their arms, which explains poor Savel's riddle which you
mentioned in your report to me. We have found stores of such arms
concealed in the church cemetery. Crepyn's death and Duket's later
murder changed everything for they brought you into this matter and
so alarmed the rebels that they hired special assassins to track you
down and kill you.*

"It would also appear, and I do not blame you for this, that Alice
atte Bowe attempted by other means to divert you from your task.
Fortunately, neither tactic succeeded. This self-confessed criminal,
Peter, also admitted that he had no knowledge of the whereabouts of
Alice atte Bowe, who had mysteriously fled the day before her
comrades were seized. However, Peter did supply us with other
names and the royal serjeants have been busy in arresting numerous
people throughout the city. One group did contrive to make a stand,
barricading themselves in a house off the Walbrook. Royal archers
fired the dwelling and cut down any who tried to escape. London has
now been purged of these vermin and safely returned to its loyalty to
our Lord the King. Consequently, I urge you to return here with all
possible speed. God save you. Written at Westminster — June
1284."*

Corbett heaved a sigh of relief. So, Alice had escaped. He
agreed with Burnell, he wanted to return and immediately
ordered a disgruntled Ranulf to pack their belongings.
Corbett took leave of the King and that same day they were
on the road south. It was strange to be free of the bustle and
noise, riding through the summer countryside. However,
Corbett felt his anxieties and fears crowding in on him
again, a feeling of deep panic which made him ride faster,
making Ranulf forget his grumbles about leaving the
new-found luxuries of the Court.

It only took them a few days to reach the outskirts of
London. Corbett decided to leave Ranulf and the horses at a
riverside inn while he hired a skiff to take him to
Westminster. He arrived there about noon on the fourth day

after he left Woodstock and, as he walked through the Great Hall, sensed danger and excitement. It was always the same after a crisis, Corbett reasoned. Warrants had to be issued; letters drawn up, judgments recorded, recognizances and testimonies witnessed and sealed. All meant an increase in the work load for the clerks who caught some of the fear, tension and excitement from the documents they handled. Corbett tried to ignore any salutations or attempts to drawn him into conversation. He wanted to see Burnell immediately, not be drawn into desultory chatter. He did note that certain of the senior clerks looked at him strangely, their eyes slipping away when he stared back.

Burnell was in his chambers but Corbett was told to wait and had to stand around for hours until the Chancellor sent for him late that afternoon. He found Burnell, still swathed in robes, almost immersed in a sea of documents which lay curled, spread and heaped across the great table. The Chancellor stared as Corbett came into the room, his dark hooded eyes carefully scrutinizing the clerk before he waved him to a stool and poured him a goblet of heavy red Gascon wine. Corbett sat down and sipped the wine, waiting for Burnell, who sat, gazing closely into his own cup, to begin.

"Master Hugh," Burnell said, putting his cup down. "The work that you did was good, very good. That nest of traitors has been netted, some were tortured and so many more have been hanged. A few," he smiled evilly at Corbett, "will be hanged by the purse. Huge benevolences. Loans to guarantee their future good behaviour. Your part in this will never be forgotten. Oh," Burnell added, almost as an afterthought. "Master Hubert Seagrave. Do you know his whereabouts?"

"Seagrave," Corbett flatly replied, "was a traitor and I have executed him. He was giving information to the highest bidder. He deserved to die!"

The Chancellor was going to speak but stopped and shuffled amongst the papers on his desk. "There was the woman," Burnell said slowly. "Alice atte Bowe, her maiden name was Fitz-Osbert. She was arrested on the Dover road by a mounted patrol and brought back to the city."

"And," Corbett heard his voice interject like ice snapping, a sound from far away.

"And what?" Burnell asked.

"The woman!" Corbett exclaimed. He could feel his heart pounding like the hooves of a charging horse. "The woman! What happened to her?" he cried.

"Oh," Burnell replied, not raising his eyes. "She was not tortured. She confessed all and then cursed us just as clearly. She was brought here before King's Bench and accused of treason, murder and witchcraft. Alice atte Bowe was found guilty and burnt at Smithfield for her crimes!"

The Chancellor's voice trailed off as Corbett sat, white-faced, his nightmares realized. He had almost prepared himself for such news and only this prevented him from giving voice to the terrible pounding in his ears and the shrill screaming in his head. Corbett was stunned. Images whirled like blazing wheels through his brain. He heard the Chancellor cough and begin speaking again.

"I am sorry, Hugh. So very sorry. I, too, found her beautiful. She left you this." He tossed a small, black, silken glove into Corbett's lap. "She gave no other message. She did not suffer," Burnell's voice slightly faltered. "I – I ensured that she did not suffer. A cup of wine, heavily drugged, was given to her before the fires at Smithfield were started."

Corbett, still dazed, heard the Chancellor's voice as if from a great distance, but he did not care. He felt the room turn and spin, his mouth was dry and he felt nauseous and weak. He rose, the small black glove clutched tightly in his hand. He heard Burnell call out but he walked from the chamber, pushing aside startled officials who might have objected but swallowed their words when they saw Corbett's harassed face.

Eventually, Corbett fought his way out of the Hall and almost ran down to the riverside wharf where, out of breath, he slumped down at the top of some crumbling weather-beaten steps. He tried to calm his breath, to still his thudding heart. Alice was gone, dead, the world was empty without her. Above him, a gull screeched against a steel-grey sky. Corbett smelt the glove, Alice's faint perfume recalling the very essence of her being. It was almost warm against the icy coldness of his face. He held the glove gently in his hand, then let it drop like some rare black flower into the river below. It bobbed, stirred, and then the current caught and pulled it. The river lapped round the glove before driving it out to the vastness of the open sea.

Author's Note

The reader may be interested in the following extract from a London chronicle written in Latin at the time. The translation runs as follows:-

"In that year Lawrence Duket, a London goldsmith, mortally wounded Ralph Crepyn in Cheapside and fled to the church of Saint Mary Le Bow. Afterwards certain evil men from the party of the said Ralph entered the church by night, killed the said Lawrence by hanging him from a window bar. A postmortem was held on this and the verdict reached that the said Lawrence had committed suicide; on account of this the body was dragged by the feet outside the city and interred in a ditch. Soon afterwards, because of the confession of a certain boy who had lain with the said Lawrence on the night of his death but then escaped, the truth of the matter came out. On account of which a certain woman, Alice atte Bowe, who was the author of this crime, together with sixteen men were imprisoned and afterwards many of these were hanged and the woman burnt. The said church was put under interdict by the Archbishop of Canterbury, the doors and windows being blocked up with thorns. Lawrence Duket was exhumed from the place where he had been buried and re-interred in hallowed ground."

Alice atte Bowe, therefore, did exist. She was the organizer of a gang or coven which committed sacrilege and murder in the church of Saint Mary Le Bow in 1284. London at that time was in the middle of political change and tumult and the crime may well have been something to do with the murky politics of the time. De Montfort was destroyed at Evesham in a bloody and barbaric way and his followers did later carry out assassinations. The church of Saint Mary Le Bow was the centre of Satanic practices, for Fitz-Osbert was a historical person, who for a short time wielded considerable political power in the capital.

MURDER WEARS A COWL

P. C. Doherty

A medieval mystery featuring Hugh Corbett

In 1302 a violent serial killer lurks in the city of
London, slitting the throats of prostitutes. And
when Lady Somerville, one of the Sisters of
St Martha, is murdered in the same barbaric
fashion, her death closely followed by that of
Father Benedict under suspicious circumstances,
Edward of England turns to his trusted clerk,
Hugh Corbett, to reveal the identity of the
bloodthirsty assassin.

Joining Corbett in his mission is his devious
manservant Ranulf, and his faithful horseman
Maltote. In the dark, fetid streets of the city and
in the desolate abbey grounds, they encounter
danger and deceit at every turn. Only Ragwort,
the mad beggar, who sleeps beneath the scaffold,
has seen the killer strike, and the one clue that
Corbett has to help him is Lady Somerville's
cryptic message: *Calcullus non facit monachum* –
the cowl does not make the monk . . .

FICTION / CRIME 0 7472 3991 6

P. C. Doherty

AN ANCIENT EVIL

THE KNIGHT'S TALE OF MYSTERY AND MURDER AS HE GOES ON PILGRIMAGE FROM LONDON TO CANTERBURY

As the travellers gather in the Tabard Inn at the start of a pilgrimage to pray before the blessed bones of St Thomas à Becket in Canterbury, they agree eagerly to mine host Harry's suggestion of amusing themselves on each day of their journey with one tale and each evening with another – but the latter to be of mystery, terror and murder. The Knight begins that evening: his tale opens with the destruction of a sinister cult at its stronghold in the wilds of Oxfordshire by Sir Hugo Mortimer during the reign of William the Conqueror and then moves to Oxford some two hundred years later where strange crimes and terrible murders are being committed. The authorities seem powerless but Lady Constance. Abbess of the Convent of St Anne's, believes the murders are connected with the legends of the cult and she petitions the King for help.

As the murders continue unabated, special commissioner Sir Godfrey Evesden and royal clerk Alexander McBain uncover clues that lead to a macabre world sect, which worships the dark lord. But they can find no solution to a series of increasingly baffling questions and matters are not helped by the growing rift between Sir Godfrey and McBain for the hand and favour of the fair Lady Emily.

'Medieval London comes vividly to life . . . Doherty's depictions of medieval characters and manners of thought, from the highest to the lowest in the land, ringing true'
Publishers Weekly

FICTION / CRIME 0 7472 4356 5

A TAPESTRY OF MURDERS

P. C. Doherty

Chaucer's pilgrims, quarrelling amongst themselves, are now in open countryside enjoying the fresh spring weather as they progress slowly towards Canterbury. A motley collection of travellers, they each have their dark secrets, hidden passions and complex lives. As they shelter in a tavern from a sudden April shower they choose the Man of Law to narrate the next tale of fear and sinister dealings.

In August 1358, the Dowager Queen Isabella, mother of King Edward III, the 'She Wolf of France', who betrayed and destroyed her husband because of her adulterous infatuation for Roger Mortimer, lies dying of the pestilence in the sombre fortress of Castle Rising, where her 'loving' son has kept her incarcerated. According to the Man of Law, Isabella dies and her body is taken along the Mile End Road and laid to rest in Greyfriars next to the mangled remains of her lover, who has paid dearly for his presumption in loving a queen. Nevertheless, as in life so in death Isabella causes intrigue, violence and murder. Nicholas Chirke, an honest young lawyer, is brought in to investigate the strange events following her death – and quickly finds himself at his wits' end trying to resolve the mysteries before a great scandal unfolds.

FICTION / CRIME 0 7472 4588 6

A Rare Benedictine

The Advent of Brother Cadfael

Ellis Peters

'Brother Cadfael sprang to life suddenly and unexpectedly when he was already approaching sixty, mature, experienced, fully armed and seventeen years tonsured.' So writes Ellis Peters in her introduction to *A Rare Benedictine* – three vintage tales of intrigue and treachery, featuring the monastic sleuth who has become such a cult figure of crime fiction. The story of Cadfael's entry into the monastery at Shrewsbury has been known hitherto only to a few readers; now his myriad fans can discover the chain of events that led him into the Benedictine Order.

Lavishly adorned with Clifford Harper's beautiful illustrations, these three tales show Cadfael at the height of his sleuthing form, with all the complexities of plot, vividly evoked Shropshire backgrounds and warm understanding of the frailties of human nature that have made Ellis Peters an international bestseller.

'A must for Cadfael enthusiasts – quite magical' *Best*
'A beautifully illustrated gift book' *Daily Express*
'A book for all Cadfael fans to treasure' *Good Book Guide*
'Brother Cadfael has made Ellis Peters' historical whodunnits a cult series' *Daily Mail*

HISTORICAL FICTION / CRIME 0 7472 3420 5

A selection of bestsellers from Headline